the Book of Michael

a novel by Lesley Choyce

Red Deer
PRESS

5 4 3 2 1

Published by Red Deer Press – A Fitzhenry & Whiteside Company
1512, 1800–4 Street S.W. Calgary, Alberta, Canada T2S 2S5
www.reddeerpress.com

Edited by Peter Carver
Cover image and design by
Jacquie Morris & Delta Embree, Liverpool, NS
Text design by Tanya Montini
Printed and bound in Canada

Financial support provided by the Canada Council, and the Government of Canada through the Book Publishing Industry Development Program (BPIDP).

Canada Council for the Arts | Conseil des Arts du Canada

Library and Archives Canada Cataloguing in Publication
Choyce, Lesley, 1951-
Book of Michael / Lesley Choyce.
ISBN 978-0-88995-417-5
I. Title.
PS8555.H668B66 2008 jC813'.54 C2008-900067-6

United States Cataloguing-in-Publication Data
Choyce, Lesley, 1951-
The book of Michael / Lesley Choyce.
[240] p. : cm.
Summary: After spending 6 months in prison wrongly convicted for the murder of his girlfriend, 16-year-old Michael Grove is released, only to find that the stigma of imprisonment will not be easy to escape.
ISBN-13: 9780889954175 (pbk.)
1. Relationships – Fiction. I. Title.
[Fic] dc22 PZ7.C5693Bo 2008

ENVIRONMENTAL BENEFITS STATEMENT

Red Deer Press saved the following resources by printing the pages of this book on chlorine free paper made with 100% post-consumer waste.

TREES	WATER	ENERGY	SOLID WASTE	GREENHOUSE GASES
22 FULLY GROWN	8,138 GALLONS	16 MILLION BTUs	1,045 POUNDS	1,961 POUNDS

Calculations based on research by Environmental Defense and the Paper Task Force.
Manufactured at Friesens Corporation

To Valerie Burke-Harland

and Peter Carver

Chapter 1

Some people still think I killed her. Despite the evidence. Despite everything.

I would prefer not to tell you this story. I am sick to death of thinking about it. I'm twenty–one now. That's supposed to mean something. That's supposed to mean I'm an adult and can leave some things from my childhood and teenage years behind. If only I could do that. Telling you this story will not give me hope or peace and it cannot make the past go away. I live with it everyday. My eyes are wide open to what happened. I can still see every detail vividly. Writing it down will not change that. It will not make me happier. But I will do this thing. I will tell my story.

"Tunnel vision" is the phrase they used to explain why I was charged, arrested, and convicted. The police investigators and the prosecution had tunnel vision. They could only see what they believed to be true.

They believed I murdered my girlfriend. They were dead certain that I killed Lisa. During the trial, I started to cry and they thought it was because I was guilty. I was blubbering and I don't think anyone could even understand what I was saying. *How can you murder someone you love?* That was what I was trying to say. No one seemed to understand that I loved Lisa so much. And then she was gone.

And it was my fault.

But I didn't kill her. I could never have harmed her.

The worst of it is this: five years after all this happened, I still miss her. I still want her to be there. What we had can never be replaced.

Tunnel vision. The law could not see that I loved her. The law could not see that it was impossible for me to do such a thing. The law saw a young man with a chip on his shoulder, an angry young man. I was that person. I was angry about a lot of things, although much of it, I think, was just being sixteen and being male. I had pushed away some people who cared about me and trained myself to be downright nasty to those I didn't like. And then the one good thing in my life was violently taken away from me.

Lisa loved me despite the anger I had in me. And I think I was changing. I was becoming a better person. A happier person.

The cops with their tunnel vision saw the way I was dressed, knew that I did drugs, smoked weed, and took some pills. They knew that I had been picked up drunk on a couple of occasions. One time I even pissed on the tires of the police car. Stupid of me, yes. But that was before Lisa. She was helping me clean up my act.

They all knew for a fact that I had had sex with Lisa. They knew this because I told the truth. I had admitted that we had made love. The prosecutor immediately rephrased *love* to *sex* and made me say that we had sex. They wanted me to say it that way. They already knew that we had sex because there was evidence. The sex part added to the tunnel vision of the law. It was as if we were the only sixteen–year–olds who were sexually active. It was as if that was all part of the crime.

And that made everything appear that much worse.

And I'm going to have to tell you about Miranda. I'm going to have to explain why Lisa's death was my fault.

I'm going to have to tell you why I feel so guilty.

The court had assigned this shrink to me, Dr. Kaufman, to do a psychological evaluation. He had the tunnel vision too. He saw everything in black and white. I'd never even met a psychiatrist before. And Kaufman was a forensic psychiatrist. Like in the TV shows. He understood nothing about me. The more I said, the more he interpreted. The more he got it wrong. And in the end used it against me. He said it was all confidential but it wasn't.

I made the mistake of telling him about the dream.

After I lost Lisa, I had the dream over and over. Lisa had breathing problems sometimes. She had asthma. When she first told me, I couldn't believe it. She was so smart and so beautiful. And so everything. I just didn't think a girl like that could have asthma. Sometimes she'd be short of breath or have a hard time breathing and she'd use one of those puffers. Sometimes when we were together, I'd carry her puffer. How's that for romantic?

So in my dream, I'm with Lisa in the forest behind her house and she starts to have problems breathing. She asks for the puffer and I can't find it. In the dream, she gasps and gasps and holds onto me and then stops breathing.

In the dream, she dies and it's all my fault.

"And you feel what?" Dr. Kaufman had asked.

"I feel fear and panic and then sadness. And guilt."

"Guilt?"

"Yes," I said.

He had recorded that conversation. It was never presented as evidence in court but then it wasn't really necessary. Kaufman interpreted my recurring dream as evidence that I had really killed Lisa but was repressing the truth, making myself believe that I didn't do the crime when in fact I had.

"You'll feel better," he said, "if you can come out and say what really happened, if you can stop covering up the truth. Admission of guilt is the first step to healing."

That was when I first began to see the possibility that I was crazy, that something in me had snapped. Maybe because of the drugs. Maybe something else. He succeeded in making me doubt myself. He succeeded in making me doubt the truth.

Until I came to the conclusion that there was no truth. Only the pain I felt in my heart. And that I wanted to die but didn't have the will to do it.

Chapter 2

I served six months in the Severton Correctional Institution. A half year is a long time when you are sixteen. It's crazy how many times when you are growing up, you use a word like "jail." "They put him in jail," you'd say about a criminal. Or about the drugs: "They'd fine you but they'd never put you in jail." Or my father talking about some corporate sleaze who was ripping off the public: "Someone should put that bastard in jail. Lock him up."

Locked up. In jail. No matter how you phrased it, that was where I was. Institution sounds grand, doesn't it? "Where's Michael?" "Oh, he's working at the Institution." Working cleaning toilets. That was my first job at the institution. That and learning who I could trust: no one. And who I needed to stay away from: just about everyone.

Correctional was the other word that didn't fit. How was I being corrected? How was I going to be punished and then fixed and then somehow let back out into the world when I was older – after my life was stolen from me?

I heard what they had said about me. There wasn't much I missed. "Lock him up and throw away the key." "He shouldn't be allowed to live." Let me remind you that I was charged and convicted of murder, but in the public mind I was also guilty of rape. I was a monster, as far as everyone was concerned. Everyone except my parents. They never stopped believing I was innocent.

My mother prayed for me through the trial and continued praying for me after I was incarcerated. I heard her prayer sometimes, or thought I did, as I lay on my bed in Severton. "Please, God, please help Michael. Please show him love and please find a way to prove his innocence. And please let him know that I still love him and believe in him. Please, God, do this."

Maybe it was God who did set me free. Something happened. Something made the true killer confess.

And my father. He lost his job. Who wants to buy insurance from a man whose son is a murderer? A murderer and a rapist?

I was destroying their lives. They were going down

with me. All we had going for us was my mother's prayers. And I didn't have much faith they would do any good.

Please, God: just let this all be over. That was my prayer. I didn't exactly know what "over" meant. Just anything that would make the nightmare stop, anything that would make the anger and the hurt go away.

I had my own "room" at the institution. The guards were supposed to watch out for me. I was at risk, they said. Suicide maybe. Or victim to some violent offender in the institution who might want to harm me. A lot of people who knew nothing about me wanted me to be beaten up. Or raped. Or murdered. Or all three in that order.

So it got me my own room. With a toilet. And a light to read by. I thought reading might save me. It helped. It made the hours of the day move along. It took me into the nighttime until I could fall asleep. I read books on religion and books about dying and the afterlife. Books about near death experience and people back from the dead and books about travel and nature. I read dozens of novels and I even read poetry.

A rapist and a murderer sitting in his cell reading Walt Whitman and William Wordsworth. And Russian novels.

It seems odd, doesn't it? Weird maybe. Crazy.

I'm trying to convey how strange it all was. I'm trying to make you understand what it was like. One day, you are sitting in French class in high school, watching the sunlight dance on the hair of a girl across the aisle from you. The hair of a girl you have fallen in love with. You are daydreaming about her, about the afternoon ahead, about the times you have kissed her, made love to her. The teacher is droning on about French verbs. The girl turns and smiles at you. You melt and die–there, I've used that word again. You die of... well... of happiness. Something so alien to your system that it makes everything seem like a fantasy. But it isn't.

A month later you realize it was a fantasy. A blip in the continuum of unhappiness leading up to pure horror.

I need to tell you as much as I can about Lisa but it has to come out in small parcels. It's too sad to tell you everything at once. I need to tell you about Miranda too and about the drugs. And about jealousy. I didn't know anything about jealousy.

I remember Dr. Kaufman asking me a question:

"When was the first time that you realized you were on the wrong path?" In life, he meant. During a session with my parents, he had asked them, "When was the first time you realized there was something... different... about Michael?" What I think he meant was, "When was the first time you realized there was something wrong with Michael?" *When did he start to turn bad?*

Maybe it was this. I was thirteen at the time. I was caught stealing cigarettes from someone's car. The window was down. They were there. I had just started smoking. Cigarettes were expensive. It was easy.

My grandmother was a smoker. My father's mother. Phyllis Grove. "Grandma" and "Granny" never fit easily, so we all called her Phyllis. Phyllis gave me my first cigarette. She was that kind of grandmother.

"Michael, you should forget about all that bullshit they say about cigarettes. There are people out there who don't want you to have any fun. Some people can't handle cigarettes. I can. I smoke four a day. No more." She held out a lit cigarette, some kind of extra–long variety. She traced her finger along the paper. "Right there. The trick is to smoke only two–thirds of the cigarette. Right to there. And then put it out. Avoid breathing the smoke when you snuff it. All the toxins stay in the last third. Forget about the filter. Filters have more chemicals in them than the tobacco. It's avoiding that last third of tobacco that will save your lungs."

I watched intently as she inhaled deeply and her eyes seemed to roll back a little as she enjoyed the smoke. Then she coughed out loud and laughed. That's what I liked best about my grandmother. Her laugh. She could laugh at anything. Any time, any place. She was a laugher.

"Your grandfather never smoked," she told me. "And he died young. He used to lecture me about smoking, about my health." The laugh again. An infection that started out as a cut in my grandfather's foot killed him when I was only nine. I missed him. So did she.

Phyllis had an unnerving habit of asking me the age–old question, "What do you want to be when you grow up?" But she said it this way: "What do you want to be when you grow up… this week?" Because I had a different answer for her each time.

At nine I wanted to be a doctor. At ten, a policeman.

At eleven, a lawyer, at twelve an oceanographer, at thirteen a doctor, at fourteen a designer of video games. Of course, there were a lot of other oddball professions in between I wanted to be but didn't really know much about. At fifteen it was starting to get fuzzy. And by sixteen, it had gone to hell. I didn't really want to grow up to be anything. But that's not quite right.

"What do you want to be when you grow up this week?"

"I want to run away with Lisa and live in a cabin somewhere in the north. I want to live alone with her. We'll grow our own food and be self–sufficient and stay there. Never set foot in a shopping mall again, never watch TV, never have to put up with people watching us."

"Is that your idea or Lisa's?"

"Hers," I admitted, but I wanted to go along with it.

Phyllis studied the nicotine stains on her index finger and thumb. My guess is that she had long since given up on the four smokes a day. "Why do you want to remove yourself from society like that?"

"Because society sucks," I said. "I watch the news. I see what's going on."

"That it does. But some of us are stuck here, I guess, trying to make the best of it."

When I was twelve, my grandmother became a criminal. She was working for a charitable organization called the United Appeal. She was a fund–raiser and a good one. So good that she decided to keep part of what she raised for herself.

"The term is embezzlement," Phyllis said, looking down. "I knew it was wrong but I did it anyway. And got caught." She let out a long sigh. "I just felt that all my life I'd never been able to buy the things I wanted. Everybody else came first. And here was this chance." She looked up at me. "I intended to pay it back and I thought I could do that before anyone would notice. But I was wrong."

Unlike me, my grandmother didn't do any time. She had to turn over the money and she had to pay a fine and see a counselor. She performed "community service," a term she loathed. "Community service, my ass," she'd say.

Phyllis gave a talk at schools about the importance of honesty. She had to repent of her crime and use herself as an example of someone who had taken the wrong path. She even spoke at my school. "That's your grandmother?"

kids would ask, incredulous. As if a grandmother could not steal from a charity.

"When your grandfather died, Michael, I felt like everything was unfair. It was like there was no justice in the world and there were no rules. I started seeing things differently. It changed me. In some ways I was better off for it." Phyllis said this to me, not to the kids in the schools. She worked hard to undo her community service when she had her heart–to–heart talks with me.

One day, less than a month before Lisa died, I was mowing my grandmother's lawn. It was a warm day and I was quite sweaty when I finished. Phyllis offered me a cigarette as usual and then a beer. "You should run away with that girl, Michael. Get the hell out of here."

"You're crazy," I said and laughed.

"Michael, the world is crazy. You'll have to work hard to hold onto your sanity."

"I don't think I could just run away."

"I know. It would break your father's heart."

But we should have run away. We should have moved up north into a cabin. It was almost like my grandmother knew something bad was going to happen.

Phyllis was the other person who never ever doubted my innocence. The trial and the publicity nearly destroyed her though. She aged ten years overnight. When I was declared guilty of murder, Phyllis stood up and cursed long and hard at the judge and jury until she was removed from the courtroom.

For three days I felt numb. I felt dead. And then the pain returned. The agony of my loss and the anger at being blamed for killing Lisa.

Chapter 3

I don't know if I can take you to the place where I existed in prison. I mean the place inside me. I don't know if anyone can understand what I felt. There was a shell I had constructed around me. I talked to almost no one. Other inmates hated me. Profound isolation is the term I came up with. Even now, five years later, I sometimes fall into that black hole inside me and have a hard time climbing back out.

There were "group" sessions with the prison psychologist, who always began the meeting with, "Who wants to go first?" We were supposed to talk about how we hurt people and how we felt about it now. It was all bullshit and everyone knew it. There was an exercise room but I couldn't handle that–the way some of the men looked at me. I talked my way out of having to go there at all.

When I was inside, reading helped keep me sane. Although sanity doesn't seem quite right. After everything that happened, I just didn't think I'd ever be right again. Reading helped some. I could sometimes live inside the books. And when I was allowed outside, always under the scrutiny of guards, I just looked up at the sky. But rather than drive us both crazy with me writing about that time, let me take you to the day when everything shifted.

It was a day like any other. I was alone but expected to go down the hall and clean up the bathroom in an hour. You can imagine how much I hated that job. The smells, the work, the humiliation. I made a point of not complaining about it, though. I had a part of me that was trying to be tough because I understood that tough meant survival in here. Why I wanted to survive, I didn't know. Some animal instinct, I suppose. Nothing more. What the hell did I have to live for?

The news arrived by way of the guard, a guy named Gus who was neither mean nor nice. Gus prided himself in being neutral and I admired him for that. He oddly always called me by my full name.

"Michael Grove," he said and I looked up from the book I was reading, Orson Scott Card's *Pastwatch*.

"Yes?"

"It's over," he said. "Come with me." He unlocked the door and walked in but I just sat there. It seemed like a scene out of a novel. Something weird was happening but I didn't know what. My first thought was that this had all been some kind of terrible dream. The nightmare was over. Or some kind of insane joke.

"What's over?"

"Your time with us," he said matter-of-factly. "You're going home."

"Tell me what's going on," I demanded. It wasn't sinking in.

"I don't really know any more than the fact that you get to leave. They didn't tell me why. Your parents are on their way. It's been nice knowing you." Again, totally deadpan. "Come on. We'll send your things along after."

"After what?"

"After you leave."

"Now?" It's odd, isn't it, that I wasn't jumping up and down, that I was confused instead. And scared. I started to cry. Gus pretended not to notice.

"You read a hell of a lot of books," he said. "Anything good?"

My eyes were somewhat out of focus. "What?" I asked.

"Any recommendations?"

"I dunno. You pick one. Take anything you want."

"Hey, thanks. Maybe I will. Now come on." He touched my arm and I almost shook him off. But I realized it was a gentle touch, or a professional one. Gus had never been a bully.

He led me through the jail and back out through the security gate. It had been almost six months to the day since I had walked through there. Six months since I had given up all hope. And now this.

My parents were waiting. My dad was crying and my mom was holding back the tears. Alongside of them was one of the administrators. I'd only seen him a few times. He was one of the people in charge here. Man in a business suit whose stock in trade was felons. Now he was losing an item in his inventory. He handed me a document–a letter or something in an envelope. "This makes it official," was all he said. "Sorry this had to happen to you."

An apology. The man was trying to apologize to me for the ruin of my life.

My father hugged me so hard I couldn't breathe and

then my mother was kissing my neck. "Let's get out of here," she said, sobbing now.

I'd like to tell you it was a happy moment. I'd like to say we walked out into bright sunlight and had a kind of celebration. But it wasn't like that at all.

It was raining. We all got wet walking to the car. I felt cold and my bones ached. I had a pain inside my chest–holding something back, I expect. Crying now but not crying. I sat in the front seat by my dad and my mom got in the back.

My father was a having a hard time driving. "Did they explain to you what happened?"

"No," I said. "I'm not really sure what's going on."

"We knew you didn't do it," my mother said. "We never gave up believing in you."

My father was crying some more and he wasn't driving very well. For some reason, that concerned me more than knowing why I was released. "They never gave you a chance," he said. "The bastards never gave you a chance."

"Calm down, Alf," my mom said. "Watch the road." The wipers were flapping back and forth. The visibility was bad. "Slow down some."

He slowed the car and peered straight ahead into the rain and gloom. There was a lot of traffic on the road. I noticed that my own breathing was funny and my hands were sweating. It occurred to me again that maybe I was dreaming. I had lost the ability to find the dividing line between what was truly real and what wasn't. That had started soon after the murder, right through the trial, and my ability to make the distinction had slipped even further away during those six months of incarceration until I played almost any scene as if it could be real or fantasy. I just wasn't sure of what was what. Maybe that's why I was not really reacting to the fact I'd been freed.

I was afraid to ask the question: "What happened?" I was afraid that once I said it, I'd receive some ludicrous explanation and it would prove this car ride with my parents was something in my imagination. And there was a bubble in my brain bursting with the possibility that someone was going to tell me this: the "mistake" had to do with Lisa. She was still alive. This was impossible but if I was in dreamland, then anything was possible. And I hungered to hear that my memory was false.

"I'm going to pull off the road so we can talk," my

father said, clearly still very shaken by the emotional impact of the day. He pulled into a Burger King but left the car running and the windshield wipers going. My dad touched my shoulder and I looked into his eyes, realizing how much of a toll all this had taken on him. My mother leaned forward and touched me on the cheek.

"It wasn't fair what they did to you," she said. "But now everything will be different."

"What changed?" I finally asked.

"Miranda Morgan. She confessed."

"Miranda?"

"You used to go out with her, didn't you?"

"Oh, my God," I said. This was the first piece to a horrible puzzle I would now have to fit together.

"They didn't even believe her at first," my father said. "They almost didn't tell us or tell anyone. They had tried you and convicted you and they wanted it closed."

"Why would Miranda do it?"

"She admitted to doing drugs. Serious stuff. Crystal methedrine."

"But that wouldn't make her kill Lisa."

"When the police told her to go home, apparently

she came back with the knife. Some dried blood was still on it. They checked the DNA."

A car stopped alongside of us in the parking lot. Two adults and three kids got out of the car. They were getting wet from the rain and the kids were giggling as they all ran for the door of the Burger King. DNA. I had come to know those as three horrible letters of the alphabet. I had been convicted by DNA. Lisa and I had made love that afternoon. My DNA proved that. The prosecutor was proud of his case, his science, his conviction.

"But why?" I asked no one.

"I don't know," my mom said. "I don't know if she said why. It must have been the drugs."

But it began to sink in. Everything about Miranda began to flood back into my memory. I opened the door and threw up on the pavement. I heaved my guts until there was nothing left and when I looked up, I saw the family that had parked alongside of us. They were at a table by the window looking out at a boy vomiting all over the tires of their car.

Chapter 4

Miranda came into my life because I wanted to be bad. When you are a teenage guy and you are heading into your bad phase, when you are pissed off at the world and want to make a statement about how screwed up it all is, when you are cynical and smart and thinking about turning dangerous, you better hope that a good friend comes along and sets you straight. Or you better hope that you run into a really intelligent and sweet girl–one like Lisa.

Unfortunately for me, Miranda came along before Lisa.

I had been doing okay in school up until that year. I hadn't really given my parents a hard time about much of anything except wanting to stay up too late and maybe hang out with the guys. (The "guys," my so–called friends who would quickly turn their backs on me after the murder. The guys who would give TV interviews for the news people and say they "could see it coming," or "he seemed like anybody else. It goes to show you can't trust anyone.")

I was reading *On the Road* by Jack Kerouac. I wanted to be a wild one like the author and his friends from that other time and place. I was listening to old Metallica and Iron Maiden. I hated most contemporary pop music–the whitey white pop stuff and the commercial black rap music too. I was independent of all that. I wore an old, beat–up, brown leather jacket and shredded jeans. I had a few piercings but it wasn't like I was a show–off. I had one tattoo on my thigh of a snake biting into a rat. I was already regretting the tattoo. But Miranda loved it when she saw it for the first time.

I didn't know where I was going with all this. I drank some beer and I scored some weed to smoke, then graduated to selling small amounts. Only to my friends or people I trusted.

That's how I met Miranda. I trusted her. She seemed… oh God, do I have to say it… she seemed very sexy and bad. And it was both of those elements that attracted me to her.

She hated her parents and, although she lived with

them, they didn't much seem to be part of her life. I envied her freedom. I knew she had had sex with a couple of guys I knew (guys I detested, actually) and I could see she liked me. I'd never had sex and I figured here was my chance with a really hot girl.

If I were really an adult, if I was like a religious type or giving a moral lecture, can you see how I could use this story? I'd say: *Can you see the pattern? Can you see what I did to myself? Can you see how easy it is to slip over to the dark side? To let Satan take over your life? To make one or two wrong turns and ruin your life?*

Maybe some day, if I live long enough, I might just do my own version of that. Or write a book about it like those other assholes who totally messed up their lives and then wrote memoirs and later showed up on *Oprah* exaggerating and lying about how really bad it was.

Only I wouldn't have to lie.

Miranda was a big mistake.

She too was not of her time and place. She wore tight black jeans. She had big hoop earrings. She had a tattoo on her ass that said, "Screw you." She had long, dark hair that fell straight to her shoulders. She wore dark mascara makeup around her eyes that made her seem dark and mysterious and, yes, dangerous.

Her father was a criminal lawyer and her mother owned a string of dry cleaning stores. They had lots of money. And absolutely no control over their daughter.

So I sold her some weed and then we smoked it after which we went downtown and–her idea–took nails and wandered down several city streets scratching the sides of cars that we figured belonged to people with lots of money. We were particularly hard on SUVs. "Only assholes drive SUVs," Miranda said. "It's not like these people need it for driving in the back woods. They drive out of their heated garages and they drive to the Gap store. They have no life. They deserve this."

They deserve this. This was one of the bitchingly illogical things that Miranda said about doing anything nasty to anyone. I know that, in her head, this is how she would have referred to the death of Lisa. *She deserved it.* Only she didn't.

I think you should know, just for the record, how quickly I fell from grace.

At twelve, I was still attending Sunday school and getting little awards for such a good attendance record. At thirteen, I was doing well in school and earning merit badges in Scouts. Like I said, I was thinking about becoming a doctor when I grew up. Or a professional hostage negotiator. At fourteen, my taste in music changed. And I was reading books and watching rented videos about young men–usually American or British, in their twenties–who took drugs, slept with hookers, and woke up feeling sick and empty. I was actually thinking that this was the life I wanted. They had it made. All that fun, all that pain. And then, telling the tale. I wanted to be like them.

I'm not saying I was corrupted by the books or the music or the movies. It doesn't really work that way, just in case you are wondering. We young men turning bad figure out how to do it one way or the other.

Miranda was my ticket. A dream come true.

I felt guilty about the automotive damage. I really did. Plain stupid. Miranda took me to a rave, even though we both agreed they were for rich loser kids. But we went anyway and took something–E, I suppose, or something someone claimed was Ecstasy. We both went out of our heads but it felt really great and, as soon as I recovered, I wanted to do it again.

We "borrowed" her father's SUV–I know, I know–when her parents were out of town and we drove way out of town into some wilderness roads, stopping only occasionally to have sex in the back seat. Or outside on the ground. And it was pretty wild.

I hate to sound like such an idiot but I have to tell you that I thought I was in love with her. "Sex is love," is the way Miranda explained it. "It's the same thing. Anyone who says otherwise is so full of bullshit that they don't deserve to live." In Miranda's book of wisdom, a lot of people didn't deserve to live.

Miranda liked stealing things from rich–ass stores. She had a credit card and could have afforded most anything and her old man would pay for it. But she liked the thrill. You've heard this one before, I know. A bit of a cliché but there it is. She didn't even mind getting caught.

There was other stuff. And if I'd had two eyes in my head, if I'd had half a brain, I could have seen that it was all bad news. *She* was bad news. She told me that she beat the shit out of another girl that she hated for being so popular. She told me this but I thought she was making it up. She told me that she had "used emotional restraint."

"Excuse me?" I asked.

"I used restraint. I could have killed her. I had a knife. But I didn't."

We were both high and I thought she was making this up. Just trying to get a reaction out of me.

"You were kind," I said (still thinking it was a joke). And I laughed.

I did a lot of laughing in those days. But it wasn't like the laughing I did in Scouts or with my parents or my friends that I used to play soccer with. Miranda had taught me this snickering nasty laugh. We were laughing at the world–how screwed up it was, how stupid people were. And it somehow signified how superior we were to all that. Superior and bad and living by our own rules. Like a modern day Kerouac, maybe, and his girl.

I'd stopped selling weed. I was a very small player and thought no one would care. But, one day, after a visit to the principal's office for a minor outburst in English class where I called Mr. Davis a bastard, I learned that the principal knew that I'd sold some grass. And that the cops knew. And even though I was only this teenage punk with some spare change from his sales, I was a link in a chain and somewhere down the line, my fun would end.

I was bad (and working hard at it) but I wasn't stupid. So I moved quickly out of retail altogether. My parents never had a clue. But certain teachers were watching me. And I drew a lot of attention to myself by the way I looked. Long scraggly hair–partially hanging in front of my face. My bad–ass clothes. My attitude.

Then one day some kids had a protest at the school–the good kids, the ones who wanted to change the world. Pen Walker, an old Scout buddy and former soccer teammate, asked me to join them.

At noon, instead of going to the cafeteria to eat lunch (or in my case, walking out into the woods to smoke a joint and a pair of cigarettes) a group of students were going to protest in front of the school with signs. The issue, according to Pen, was that the school was buying supplies from a corporation that was importing them from Indonesian factories where children were used as cheap labor.

Why I was supposed to give a rat's ass about this, I don't know. Maybe one part of me had been brainwashed during all those Sunday school sessions into thinking that I was supposed to support good causes.

"We need your help," Pen said.

"Why?" I asked.

"A lot of kids think you're cool."

I looked at Pen, the quintessential nerd. I was impressed that he was willing to make some noise and break some rules, and I had to give him some credit for that. Cool was not a word in my vocabulary but I understood his point. A bunch of clean-cut geeks and nerds with placards looks somehow not right. I would spice things up. I would draw attention to the event.

"You'd be helping to bring an end to sweat-shop abuse and child labor in the Third World," Pen said.

"Bite me," was my conditioned response to such bullshit. But I volunteered anyway because I knew Pen and his weak posse of noodles needed me. And because I thought it would be fun.

I don't know where Miranda was. I suppose she had other business during that noon hour. I knew she'd been moving into some other recreational drugs. She was always two steps ahead of me. She didn't seem to have any emotional baggage or any ties to old girlfriends from the past. She danced to the beat of her own loud drummer. And I knew if I ever really tried to keep tabs on her it would piss her off. And who knows what she'd do then?

So I demonstrated, had my little sign… what was it? *End Child Labor.* One buddy had a sign that simply said: *Think about who made your pencils.* That one made me laugh. There were about twenty of us. It was all very, very lame walking back and forth there on the sidewalk with a bunch of other kids laughing at us and the principal, Mr. Tyson, just poking a look out between the blinds in his window.

What was a fella to do? I figured I had no choice, and if we were going to save some little bastards from such hard work in Asia, we had to get more serious.

"Let's go out into the street and stop traffic."

Which we did. Amazingly, the nerds followed their bad–ass guru. We took it to the streets. Well, one street anyway. Twenty dweebs and a young guy who looked–to some, I reckon–like a young Charlie Manson. Cars squealed to a halt. Angry drivers yelled at us. This felt much better. Most students stood on the sidelines and egged us on–kind of like they used to do when two grade school idiots got into a fist fight. I saw Miranda now and I waved for her to join us, but she shook her head no. I could see from the look in her eyes she was really buzzed.

But you can see that by now I had the audience I wanted. And I wasn't going to take up the chant about pencils and office supplies. "Save the Children!" was my first shout. And that felt pretty good. We were standing in the street with our placards and we'd stopped the midday traffic. It was only a matter of time before someone got real pissed off and started beating on us. And I couldn't wait to see a nerd or two get wonked. But I was preparing for a quick exit when the time came.

More car horns, a few more students joined us. One of them, I realized in retrospect, was Lisa. Maybe that was the first time I really noticed her. I'd seen her around but she had always been somehow distant and aloof. And she'd never given me the time of day.

The principal was out of the school now and talking on a cell phone.

"Screw the school!" I shouted, looking right at him. "Screw the corporation!"

I don't know which corporation. Any one would do, I suppose. It was the verb that mattered. Some of the other students looked at me like I was crazy. I noticed Lisa now and her look said the obvious: *tone it down.*

"The greedy bastards!" I yelled louder.

And that's when the police arrived.

Ten of the demonstrators dropped their signs and left. Pen looked at me as if expecting me to know what to do. Four cops were out of their cars and walking towards us, towards me.

I'd learned one thing about being bad. Sometimes you didn't have to do anything. You could just stand there and pose. Even if you were gutless, even if you didn't have a cool bone in your body. People were easily impressed or intimidated just by the way you looked–if you looked like me back then. I shot a glimpse at Miranda who was looking at me. She licked her lips in a very sexy way.

A few more cops had arrived and they were holding nightsticks but trying to be very calm. Those of us who had not fled were actually standing within a circle of policemen. There was obviously nowhere to go. Pen was looking at me like I was the one who should say something. It was now *my* demonstration. I looked over and saw Lisa then and was shocked that she was still here.

A thick–necked officer stepped forward and looked at me. "What's this about?" he said in a calm voice.

That's when I spit in his face.

Chapter 5

They arrested me and only me. And claimed that spitting in a policeman's face was "assaulting an officer of the law."

"How stupid can you get?" my father screamed at me when we got in the car to go home.

"Screw you," I told him. I'd never talked like that to my father and should have realized I'd turned some dark corner. I was really heading down the back alley now. No more Sunday school attendance prizes, no merit badges. But I had decided I was another rebel with a cause. *What about those kids in sweatshops, anyway? Who the hell else was going to stand up for them?*

The truth was I didn't really do a lot of thinking about global issues or social problems. I was young and angry and any reason for my rage would do. The truth was it was all about me. Not kids in the Third World or any other world.

That night I was supposed to stay in my room, but

I sneaked out of there as I'd done before and I went over to Miranda's house. Her parents were gone. She gave me a pill of something–something she didn't even know the name of. She took some too and we got high in a weird space–cadet kind of way. Then we had sex there on the living room floor. I don't think either one of us cared if anyone would have walked in on us, but that didn't happen. It was great and she dug her nails into my back until I was bleeding.

And she bit my tongue and made that bleed too.

Afterwards, she put a frozen pizza in the microwave and it hurt to eat because of her biting my tongue. But I didn't say that. The weird stone from the pill kind of had control of me and I started talking–saying anything that came into my head.

"Pretty soon something big is going to happen. All those self–righteous shits like that cop, and Mr. Guy Tyson, and all those asshole teachers, and all the narrow–minded shitty adults who live in this town. They're gonna wake up one day and find they are on the bottom, not the top. The world is gonna turn upside down and they won't know what walloped them. They won't be able to figure out that it's me spitting in their face."

Miranda laughed and I thought she looked really cute and really sweet and I was still glowing (even while I ranted) about the fact that I'd just had sex with her, so I said, "I love you."

"Sex is love, love is sex," she answered. "I love you too." But there was no real heart to the words. They were just words. "Let's do it again."

It. Again.

Afterwards, she said she wanted to show me something and she led me to her father's home office. He had a big oak desk and all kinds of weird stuff hanging on the walls–carvings and paintings and even some small stone sculptures that looked like they could have been ancient. "My father is a collector," she said. "Look at this."

On a table was a rack with an array of oddly shaped knives. "Ceremonial knives from different cultures around the world," she explained.

"What's he do with them?"

"Nothing, silly. He collects them, remember? For my father, it's all about ownership. He likes to possess things. It makes him feel important." She suddenly ran to the door and turned off the light switch. The room went black. Then, just as quickly, she turned on the desk lamp and it cast a weird, eerie light on her. She was standing right in front of me now with a golden curved knife, holding it above her like she was ready to attack me. It scared the shit out of me. I took a step backwards and fell over a chair and ended up on the floor.

Miranda was laughing now. My heart was beating wildly.

"It was a joke," she said, putting the knife down on the desk and helping me up.

I was out of school for a week. Tyson had suspended me. My teachers expected me to "keep up with the work," which I intended to ignore. I stayed home and watched TV, fooled around on the Internet and got bored, finally started reading a book that my grandmother had given me. It was an English translation of the Chinese *I Ching*. I didn't get it at all at first. Something about divining your future by tossing sticks and interpreting them. Phyllis said the book had helped her when her life got complicated or difficult.

By my third day of suspension I was bored out of my

gourd. I would open the book to a random page and read what it had to say for Hexagram 28: *Stubbornness will bring you alienation from your true source of help and support.*

This was wonderful news. I flipped the pages to another hexagram: *Using force will lead to failure. Avoid impulsive behavior.*

Me, impulsive?

I phoned Miranda's cell phone. It rang.

"I'm in class. I can't talk," she said.

It was against the school rules to leave your cell phone on or answer it in class. A lot of kids broke that rule.

"Come over. After class. I'm going crazy."

"I can't," she said and hung up.

I made a sandwich, watched some really bad TV, gave up and flipped open the *I Ching* again. Hexagram 37: *Love develops where there is mutual trust and respect.*

Love equals sex, sex equals love, I heard a voice in my head say.

I phoned my grandmother. "Phyllis, I don't know about the book. I don't think that I'm ready for all this old Chinese bullshit."

"It's only bullshit if you insist it is bullshit."

"What is that? Hexagram 41?"

"Ah, so you are reading the book?"

"I've dipped into it. I just don't think it has anything to do with me. The world has changed. The rules are all new."

"The world hasn't changed," she said. "Why aren't you in school?"

I explained my situation.

"Your grandfather was a policeman when he was young."

"I remember him telling me. There was a story about breaking up a union strike. Someone got hurt."

"Yes. He realized he was on the wrong side. The police were breaking up the strike. He hit some of the strikers and then quit his job after that and became a union organizer. He'd be interested, if he were alive, to hear your story. I'm not sure about the spitting though. I've always thought spitting is vulgar."

"I'll try to be more polite next time."

"Whatever has been lost will return when the time is right."

"What?" I asked.

"Hexagram 38."

"Great."

"Would you like me to come over?"

I thought of my grandmother having to take two busses to where I lived. "No, it's okay. I'll just read the book. Do you miss him?"

"Who?"

"My grandfather."

"Every day. He always stood by me when I did something stupid. Even when it was so embarrassing."

"Why do you think he did that?"

"It was his nature."

"I'll call you tomorrow, Phyllis."

"Good."

Hearing my grandmother talk about my grandfather left me feeling sad. Being home alone made me feel like I'd been abandoned and cut off from the rest of the world. I opened the book again to another interpretation of Hexagram 38: *When you are alone, it is easy to mistrust even the good people.* That spooked me a bit. I felt like my grandmother was still talking to me through the words of the *I Ching* somehow.

And then the doorbell rang.

It was Lisa Conroy.

"I was sitting across from Miranda," she said. "I heard you on the cell phone. I thought you might need some books."

The charges were soon dropped–after my father's lawyer did some talking, after I promised to stay out of trouble, after I apologized to the cop. That was tough. And it was bullshit. I had liked spitting in his face–especially in front of the kids at school. And now I had something I had to live up to.

Chapter 6

The morning of my release, it took a lot of courage to simply get out of the car and go into the Burger King bathroom to clean myself up. Six months away from the world and somehow it all felt different. I felt like a person from another planet. People stared at me–it could have been my imagination, but I doubt it. My picture had been everywhere in the papers. And on television.

The words my mother had said seemed impossible. Miranda had killed Lisa. She had destroyed my life. I locked myself in the bathroom and splashed water onto my face. Then I stared into the mirror. My mind froze.

I stood like that for ten minutes. Then someone was knocking at the door. It was my father. "Michael, are you all right? Michael?"

I unlocked the door. He saw the look on my face and took me in his arms, hugged me, then led me through the restaurant and back out to the car.

When I got home, I went to my room and slept. I slept through the afternoon and through the night. I know my parents came in to check on me, but I didn't acknowledge them. I felt like Lisa had died a second time and I felt yet again, but even more painfully so, that it was my fault.

When I finally woke it was morning. Early morning. I felt disoriented but part of me felt good. It was good to be alive. I dressed, went downstairs, and walked out the back door into the backyard. The sun was out. There were birds singing. My mother's flowers were blooming. It was as if nothing had changed. Life really had gone on without me. If Miranda had not confessed, all this would have continued on. Without me. I felt isolated and insignificant. But it still felt good to be alive. Good to be free.

Free. As soon as my mind grabbed onto that word, I became confused. What did freedom mean? Could I ever really feel free again? Could I ever stop thinking about Lisa? It would always be there and so would the emerging truth about her death. And all the punishment that had been wrongfully done to me. I could never be free.

I walked out into the yard and, over the fence, I saw

our neighbor, Sutherland "Sudsy" Pinter. Sudsy had gone to school with my father. They used to be friends. But the trial changed all that. Now he was staring at me. I stared back. That's when he turned and walked back into his house. He didn't wave, he certainly wasn't smiling and he had that look–he still had that look, the one I had seen on so many faces. Pure hatred. For him, nothing had really changed. He must have known why I was home, why I was released. But he was not about to let go of his contempt for me. This is what it was going to be like, I realized.

I walked around the backyard and stopped by the maple tree. Although the tiny crosses were long gone, I knew that this was the place where I had buried our pet canary, my hamster Hughie, Ginger the family dog I had grown up with, and, most recently, Cassidy, my pet white rat. Sudsy had complained, I remember, about us burying the dog in the backyard. Sudsy was unemployed off and on and he was a real pain in the ass when he didn't have a job. Always in other people's business. Always having opinions, always mouthing off to my parents about something that was up his ass.

I picked up a Y–shaped branch that had broken off the

tree and I pushed it into the soil, a new marker for my pets. And I guess I just stood there and started to cry again. I cried for me and for the dead animals and for Lisa. And for all the sadness and hurt in the world that was inside of me. And I was sure it would never go away.

My mother came out in her housecoat and found me standing there. She collected what was left of me and took it inside the house. She made me breakfast without saying anything and then my father arrived. He was dressed for work. At first I was shocked. It seemed way too normal. But I didn't want to say anything about it. I knew they were trying to make everything seem like it used to be. I would fake it.

"How are things at the office?" I asked matter-of-factly.

He turned away and went to the coffee maker and poured himself a cup. "Um… things have changed."

"Oh," I said.

"Your father's changed jobs," my mom said.

I looked at my father's back. "Wow. You were there for… what?… like ten years."

"It was time for a change. I got tired of the insurance game."

"You never told me you changed jobs."

"Sorry about that," my mom said but nothing more. It began to sink in.

"They fired you, didn't they?"

"Not really. I decided to leave on my own."

"And now?"

"Now I'm at a call center."

"You what?"

"I answer people's complaints about their cell phones."

"Jesus. Dad."

"It's not so bad. But I'm still kind of new there. I wanted to stay home today but I've already taken time off. I really should be there today."

"It's okay," I said. "I'm okay. We're all okay."

But I knew my dad had lost his job because of me. And it wasn't like his old boss was going to call him up now and say: *Oh, we're sorry. Your son wasn't guilty after all, so you can have your old job back.*

My mom poured his coffee into a travel mug and handed him a paper bag that must have had a sandwich in it. I hadn't seen her do that since I was in grade school and she used to pack a lunch for me. She kissed him and he turned back to me. "See you when I get home. It's good to have you back." And he was gone.

I stared at my eggs and toast for a few minutes until the silence made my mom uncomfortable. She sat down across the table from me. "You don't like it?"

I hadn't tasted it yet. "In the backyard," I said. "I saw Sudsy looking at me. He looked at me like I was still guilty. Like nothing has changed."

"Sudsy Pinter is an asshole," my mother said.

I couldn't believe my mother used those words. I dropped my fork and smiled, I think, for the first time since I'd come home.

"People sometimes believe what they want to believe," she said. "Dr. Kaufman called. He was trying to be helpful. He said that some people would act this way. Once an idea is fixed in their heads, the facts won't change anything. He said we should maybe go see him if we wanted to. You and me and your father."

I shook my head. "Dr. Kaufman believed I was guilty. He took notes about everything I told him and he made his own interpretations. He was one of them. He was like Sudsy, an asshole who believed what he wanted to believe.

I'm not going back to him."

"He apologized."

"He should lose his job. He could have helped me. But he helped them."

"You're right," she said. "But you're going to need help."

"I don't want his apology and I don't want his help. I want my life back."

My mom did a good job of not crying then. Maybe she was all cried out. Maybe six months of crying had injured her tear ducts or something.

"How's Grandma Phyllis?" I asked.

"Better," she answered. "She's been in the hospital but she's home now."

I stared at her. "More secrets withheld from me."

My mom put her hands in the air. "You know Phyllis. She made me promise not to tell you. But she's okay."

"What was it?"

"Her lungs. Emphysema."

"Right," I said. And I craved a cigarette just then for the first time in a couple of months. Despite what the other inmates were doing, while inside I had stopped smoking and stopped everything. No drugs. No drinking.

I had become clean and sober, as they say. But right then I was thinking that I really wanted a smoke. And I craved a little buzz from a joint. And a beer for breakfast wouldn't be a bad thing. But I kept my mouth shut.

"I wanna go visit Phyllis," I said. "I want to go see her today."

"I'll drive you."

"No," I said. "I want to go on my own."

Chapter 7

It was a kind of test. Going out in broad daylight. Taking a bus. I wasn't really prepared for it. I wasn't really prepared for anything. But I decided to go anyway. I just knew that my parents were going to try to protect me and I didn't want that right now. I wanted to know how many people out there were going to act like Sudsy. How many never changed their minds about what they thought of me even after the truth was out.

The bus stopped and I got on, dropped my money in, and walked towards the back. I looked straight ahead and didn't make eye contact. As they say on the old *Star Trek* reruns, "Shields up." Being inside had trained me quite well at keeping to myself and ignoring whatever was going on around me. I was thinking this might be a way to get through the days ahead–or the life ahead.

Some of them were looking at me. I didn't look back. I took a seat by myself and stared out the window.

We passed through the familiar landscape of my home-town and I remembered riding my bike through these streets. So long ago. If I squinted I imagined I could see myself–Michael Grove at ten riding his twenty–one speed bike, helmet on, braking at stop signs, then riding on, the wind in his face. Riding to the library or to play soccer or to a friend's house.

What happened to all those childhood friends anyhow?

What had happened was that I inched away from them. Or pushed them away. I had lost interest in sports and games and got serious. I worked at proving how tough I could be. And bad. Where did that come from? Who put it in my head?

I was pretty certain I did it to myself. I did it because I was bored with the old me. Wasn't that what kids complained about all the time? How freaking boring everything is. School. Teachers. Books. Life. I wanted to make life more interesting.

And then Miranda came along.

A shudder went through me. I held my arms around myself to stop it. I looked at my reflection in the glass. And just then realized how much I hated my life and hated myself.

"Yo," someone said. I ignored the voice.

"Yo," he said again. I turned. Across the aisle and back sat a black man in some kind of uniform. At first, it made me think of the guards, but then I realized it was something a mechanic wore. He had his name stitched over the pocket: *Louis.* I guess I was staring at him now. "You all right?" Louis asked.

I unhugged myself and shook my head. "No. I'm not all right. But thanks for asking."

"Anything I can do?"

"Fix my life. Take me back in time."

He didn't blink. "Right now or later?" He seemed dead serious.

I laughed. "Right now would be just fine."

Louis moved up one seat but stayed on the other side of the aisle. "I know who you are now. You're that kid who..." He let the words trail off.

"Yeah, I'm that kid."

"And you didn't do it?"

"I'm not sure it matters much. My life is pretty well ruined."

He nodded. "Been there. Done that."

"No, man. Not this version, you haven't. You maybe watched something like it on TV. You didn't live it."

He scratched his cheek. "Okay. Maybe I didn't get the full meal deal you did. I read the papers. I know what I thought to be true like everybody else. And then, wham, that girl comes clean. Anybody say they were sorry?"

"Not really. Everybody thinks they were just doing their job."

"You gonna sue their asses?"

"Lawyers and judges and courtrooms again? I don't think so."

Louis rubbed his fingers together. "Somebody should pay."

"I can't think about that. Not now."

"Did you love her?"

"Yes."

"I lost someone I loved," Louis said. "My wife. It's been a while."

"Does the hurt go away?"

"Shit, no. It fades a little. It hides for a time and then it ambushes you all over again."

"Thanks for the heads up."

"You got anyone to talk to?"

"My parents think I should go back to the shrink that helped convict me."

"Screw the shrinks. Like you said, they just do their job."

I was trying to figure out something about the way he was looking at me. At first I thought maybe he was gay and trying to pick me up. Inside, I figured out that everyone had a motive. If someone was kind, they were doing it to get something. If they were mean, it was to get power. If they were trying to be invisible like me, they were trying to protect themselves. What was it with this guy? Then it clicked. "You ever been arrested?"

"Uh huh."

"Spend some time?"

"Bingo."

"But you didn't kill your wife?"

"Thought about it once or twice but I loved her. After the accident, though, I went crazy."

"How many different shades of crazy are there?" I asked.

It was an odd thing to say. He cracked a smile. "This is my stop coming up. Listen, I'm probably no help at all to you. But I'm Louis, like my label says. I always wanted a shirt with my name on it, as you might guess. Work at the muffler shop there on the corner. Come check out my shade of crazy sometime if you want to talk."

He nodded and walked down the aisle. I wondered if I looked him up in the newspaper archives, what his story would be. What version of crazy put him behind bars?

I continued to stare out the window at the once familiar landscape that now seemed like it was alien territory. At the corner, I looked down Engel Street. The high school was down there two blocks away. And it suddenly occurred to me that it was a school day. My old friends and classmates were in school. Life had gone on without me. Without Lisa. That's how it worked. Once you were removed from the picture, everyone was shocked but, after a while, things just picked up where they left off. Without you.

My grandmother did not come to the door when I rang. I could hear music and I thought I heard a voice say something, but it didn't sound like her. I opened the door and poked my head in. "Phyllis? It's me," I said.

"In the living room," she said. Her voice sounded

weak. I walked into the living room. Phyllis was sitting in a La–Z–Boy tilt back chair with a small mask over her face. Alongside her was an oxygen bottle and a tube was attached to the mask. Phyllis was clicking a remote aimed at the stereo but it wasn't working. I recognized the music–old Neil Young. Finally, the sound of the music diminished and Phyllis got up out of her chair. She took off the mask and pulled me to her. "Michael. Good to have you back. I missed you so."

I hugged her back and felt how frail she'd become. She'd changed while I'd been gone. No one had told me she needed to live with an oxygen tank and a mask. I had to try really hard to keep from crying. Once again I realized how terribly my life had been interrupted, never to be the same again. "I missed you too, Phyllis," I said.

She sat back down and I sat on a footstool in front of her. She saw the concern in my eyes.

"It's not as bad as it looks. The only real problem is I can't smoke. They say that if I light up near this thing, I'll blow up the house. I haven't decided if it would be worth a try but I'm thinking about it."

"Are you okay?" I asked.

"Hell, yes. This is nothing. It's like a holiday vacation. Me sitting here sucking pure oxygen listening to Crazy Horse."

"Some of Neil's best work."

"Damn straight. 'Cowgirl in the Sand.' 'Down by the River.' 'Last Trip to Tulsa.' All classics. They don't write songs like that anymore."

I knew all my grandmother's old favorite music. Neil Young and Crazy Horse, Buffalo Springfield, Frank Zappa, early Jefferson Airplane. I looked up at the stereo on the shelf. "*You* have an MP3 player?" I asked incredulously.

"Just trying to keep up with things." Then she let out a big sigh, took a hit of the oxygen from the mask, but then set it on her lap. "Michael, I never gave up on you."

"I know."

"Neither did your parents."

"I know that too."

"I kept thinking there must be something I could do to help you. But there wasn't."

"You sent letters."

"Words. Mere words. What was it like?"

"Well, I stopped smoking."

She looked a little embarrassed. "Jesus. I guess the

thing about smoking two–thirds didn't work. Look at me. I still got cravings. Want some gum?"

"No thanks. I went cold turkey. On everything. Thanks for the *I Ching* stuff."

"Did it help?"

"Nothing much helped but I memorized some of the lines. Here's my favorite: *Misfortune can no longer be avoided. It has to be endured.*"

"Hexagram 23. Not one of my favorites, for sure. What else went with it? *Splitting apart results in the growth of new fruit from the disintegration of the old.* Speaking of the disintegration of the old. Look at me."

"You look great." But she didn't. Phyllis looked pale and tired. But I felt a little better in her presence.

"Bag of bones. They think I'll get my lungs back, though. I've got some medication and pretty soon I'm going to start going back to the casino. If the meds don't work, I guess I'll just sit here and work on my Darth Vader imitations."

I laughed just then. Leave it to Phyllis to cut through my gloom. The very sound of my laughter seemed so strange. When was the last time I laughed?

"What are you going to do now?" Phyllis asked.

"I don't know."

"You need to go back to school."

"I don't think I can do that."

"So what's the alternative?"

"Leave," I blurted out. "Just disappear from here. Go some place."

"I know that feeling. But you can't do that to me. Or your parents."

"Wouldn't it be easier on everyone?"

"No. We all feel like we failed you already."

"None of this was your fault."

She had to take a breath from the oxygen mask then. "Well, somehow it feels like it was our fault. We let the law, the system, punish you for something you didn't do."

I shook my head and felt my eyes stinging again. "I don't know what to do with the way I feel. I hate it."

"How do you feel?"

I shook my head and did not look up. "I feel like killing someone."

"As you should. Who? The girl?"

"Strangely enough, no. I hate her for what she did.

But I know it had something to do with me. I was attracted to Miranda first. Before Lisa. I'm in there. I'm part of this."

"But you didn't want any harm to come to anyone."

"I loved Lisa. I really did. That's what is destroying me. I'll never have her again."

Phyllis kept the mask on. "And now you have to get on with your life. *Going forward with caution will produce good results*."

"Thirty-four, right? *Ta Chuang*."

"You did have a lot of time on your hands, didn't you? What was it like in there?"

"Lonely. I got over the fear. In fact, I felt strangely protected. I'm not saying bad stuff didn't happen, but I worked hard at my isolation. And it helped protect me. I didn't allow myself to get drawn into other people's dramas."

"You survived. You're tough."

"Out here, I don't think isolation and being tough are going to be enough. I feel like I have more enemies out here than back in there."

"And so you need allies. I'm one. And your parents."

"I know. But first I think I need a place to hide."

"Hide here," she said. "But you have to do me a favor first."

"Sure."

"Take some money off the table in the kitchen. Go to the corner store and buy me some lottery tickets. *Adversity creates a playing field for good luck.*"

I gave her a goofy smile. "I don't remember that one."

"That's 'cause I just made it up. From *The Wisdom According to Phyllis.*"

Chapter 8

I blew ten dollars on lottery tickets for my grandmother. The man behind the counter at the store didn't recognize me. And that was comforting. He had a little TV on behind the counter and was watching a rerun of *Friends*. Despite the laugh track, he was taking the show very seriously.

Aside from winning a few more free tickets, Phyllis had never won anything from all her lottery investments. She called it her "losing streak." It had lasted for well over ten years and that's why she was confident that the odds were good that she would win any day now.

Odds. Chance. Luck. If I thought too long and hard about it, I'd say I was up there with being one of the unluckiest people on the planet. But at least I was alive. Walking back to my grandmother's house, I couldn't envision what I wanted to do with the rest of my life. Or even the rest of my day.

It had been almost a year and a half now since Lisa's

death. The months leading up to the trial were excruciating. And before the trial was over, I knew they were going to convict me. Everyone knew. It became clear to everyone how things *appeared*.

How do you plead?

Not guilty.

And then, after all the agony, the trial came to an end. And the jury found me guilty. There were no other suspects. The prosecutor's words. *No one else could have possibly done this.* The jury's vote was unanimous. And at that moment which I had already prepared myself for, all I could think about was Lisa. How much I loved her and how much I wanted her back.

My grandmother had changed clothes and was seated at the kitchen table when I returned. There were two beers on the table. One was open and she was sipping from it. She'd put on makeup and was wearing jeans and a sweatshirt with the words, *Fools Rush In*. I'd seen her wearing it before and never really understood it. "You buy me any winners?"

I placed the lottery tickets on the table in front of her. "If I did we have to split it." It was an old routine.

Half of zip is almost always zip.

"Sixty–forty," she said.

"Okay. But only because you're my grandmother."

"Sit."

I sat and stared at the beer. She reached over and cracked the pop top. I wasn't sure it was a good idea. Mr. Clean and Sober. What the hell. I reached for the can and took a slug. It tasted good. Too good. Good old Phyllis.

"Tell me about Miranda," she said.

"Why?"

"I dunno. I want to understand this. I want it to make sense."

"Nothing makes sense."

"Yes. Strangely enough, events have meanings. They may not be meanings that are good or ones we like, but we need to try to understand."

"I told you once about Miranda–way back, remember?"

My grandmother had picked up a pencil, not to write with or anything, just to hold between the index and middle finger of her right hand like a cigarette. I noticed that she even took a breath like she had just inhaled smoke and then slowly breathed out pursing her lips together like smokers do. "I remember you being all excited about her. She was sexy and she was smart–or at least you thought so. And you were horny."

I almost blushed. "Jesus, other kids' grandmothers don't talk like that."

"Well, that's them. This is me. So, tell me more."

"She was the first one I'd had sex with. That was a big deal for me."

"Always is. First time. A girl like that would have some real power over you."

I took another sip of beer and remembered. No, I wasn't going to paint all the lurid details for Granny Phyllis. I wouldn't let it get that weird. But I couldn't help remembering. It was in Miranda's bedroom. Her parents were gone for the weekend again. We'd been making out, I'd been lying on top of her, clothes on, grinding. Then she sat up and said, "Take your pants off."

Phyllis must have noticed I was drifting. "They don't make beer as good as what your grandfather made. He made his own beer–dark. It would knock your socks off."

"Really?"

"Really. Now back to your story. I can tell you're

going to bypass all the steamy sex stuff because I'm your sweet old grandmother. That's understandable. So I'll just assume you two went at it like rabbits when you could. But there was more."

"I knew I was kind of in over my head with her. She was unpredictable, and she could be cruel. But to be perfectly honest, I was attracted to that too. I wanted to be like that."

"I always told your parents that you'd rebel against all that Sunday school and Boy Scout crap. So this was it. And drugs, right?"

"That's where it got messy." I paused and didn't know if I should go on. Phyllis saw the guilty look on my face.

"Michael. Like I said, I want to understand. And maybe, just maybe, I can help you understand. It's either me or that asshole psychiatrist."

I had been afraid to say too much out loud. Afraid to confront the chain of events that was so shadowy in my mind, but so persistent. "Okay," I said, looking down at the kitchen table. "It went something like this. We'd both toked often. Seemed we almost always had good weed. Money wasn't an issue. Then she got me to try coke. I think she stole it from her father. We'd do some coke and then..."

"And then... sex... right?"

"Yeah... well. There was that. And she'd come up with some kind of pills. Half the time she didn't know what they were. Some did nothing, some were way too weird for me and I started to back off. When I started to back off, she'd get mad. Sometimes she'd hang out with other friends of hers. Creeps I didn't like. I didn't really know them. They didn't go to our school. I mean, they weren't like Satan worshippers or anything, just creepy not nice people."

Phyllis let out a small laugh. "Sorry... it was the 'not nice' phrase. Go on."

"I'd heard about crystal meth but never tried it. When Miranda told me it was the best stuff yet, I tried it but pretty soon I had to draw the line."

"I read about the stuff. Seems to me you did the right thing."

"She took it as a kind of betrayal, I think. I kept seeing her and sometimes she was on the stuff. You'd never know what she was going to do next. I was thinking I was in too deep over my head but..."

"I know. But the sex was too good."

"Well, I didn't want to come out and say it. But that was a pretty big part of it. And I *thought* I was in love with her."

"Love takes many forms. Maybe you were. Don't deny yourself that. But something changed the way you felt… despite the great sex, right?"

"Do you remember the demonstration?"

"The one where you spit at a cop?"

"In his face, actually. Totally, totally stupid on my part. I got carried away."

"I've been in demonstrations. People tend to get carried away."

"Lisa was there in the crowd. I barely knew her before that. She was sincere about the issue. I was just along for the ride. But when I found myself face to face with that cop, I felt this power."

"You felt self–righteous. And you thought you could get away with anything. What about Miranda?"

"She was on the sidelines. She didn't get involved at all. Weird, eh?"

"Not weird. Miranda was about Miranda. Not saving children from slavery."

"It was after that that Lisa paid attention to me. We became friends at first. She was into issues–global warming, animal rights, gun control. You name it and she was either for or against it in a major way. And she was a whole lot less complicated than Miranda."

"And she was cute?"

"Not like Miranda. She didn't try to make herself look sexy. But she was. I didn't even notice it at first. And then it started to sink in."

"And then came the sex?"

"Well, yeah. But not before I'd told Miranda it was over."

"What did Miranda say?"

"She was high at the time. Not sure on what. I thought she'd scratch my eyes out. I was prepared to run. Really. Instead, she acted like it was no big deal. Said she was already thinking about moving on. I was too tame, she said. Not willing to push the envelope."

"But she didn't let it go, did she?" Phyllis took another drink of beer.

"I never knew," I said. "And that's the part that's driving me crazy. I would have never believed it. Until the truth came out. Until she confessed."

"Michael, I'm so sorry. I wish I could make the hurt go away."

"I don't think anyone can do that," I said.

Chapter 9

Phyllis looked tired and sad now. "I have to go plug myself back in," she said.

I guess I must have looked puzzled.

"The oxygen bottle."

I tried to help her stand up but she brushed me away. I followed her back into the living room. "I'm gonna rest awhile. You go home. Give yourself some time to adapt. And don't take any crap from the assholes out there."

I knew which assholes she was talking about and her phrasing was quintessential Phyllis. My grandmother, even when I was little, would shock my friends or their parents at occasions like school graduations or birthday parties. She always spoke her mind freely.

The first bus on my way home did not stop. I was waiting alone and it slowed but then it just kept on going. I tried not to make too much of the possibilities. I decided to walk the first leg of the trip back home. As

I started the hike, I listened to my breathing and remembered lying on my bunk back inside Severton. I had trained myself to steady my breath, follow it with my mind, and put myself into a state of meditation. Like reading books, it was one of those things that kept me from going insane.

Given my circumstances, I was beginning to believe that I had survived amazingly well in prison. I'm not saying it was good, I'm just saying I'm surprised. The conviction was one thing. That was when the numbness began to set in. Part of me is still not over that even now, years later. But the times, they were a–changing, as Bob Dylan would say. I was guilty, the jury had determined, of murder, and many people still believed I raped her. And I was sixteen. I was tried as an adult. That was nothing new. But I was sentenced as an adult too. That was rare. And that decision scared the crap out of my parents.

"Young offender" is the term used to debate this issue in the papers. Not long before my case, a young offender with a long list of crimes had stolen a car and killed a woman with it. There was an inquiry into the whole thing and it was determined that the law needed to deal more harshly with violent young offenders. Circumstance and history had delivered me into that spotlight. If a sixteen–year–old commits a murder, do you send him to the youth correctional facility or do you send him to adult prison?

It was a hypothetical question up until my trial came along. But the judge determined that I was to be deemed an adult, that I would have to take adult responsibility for what I'd done. Only problem was that I hadn't done anything. My lawyer, Joshua Hawker, unfortunately for me, was not very popular with the press. He had, it turned out, defended real murderers before and got them off on technicalities that allowed them to go free, including one man who murdered again. My father had picked Hawker against my mother's wishes. My father's lawyer had said, "Hawker is the best."

Well, yes and no. In my case, no.

Hawker "coached" me about how to present myself in court. I hated it. It all seemed so false. The point was I didn't do it. Up until the first few days of the trial, I believed that my innocence would be obvious. But it wasn't. The circumstances made it look like I killed Lisa. "The jury will take one look at you and want to believe you are guilty," Hawker told me. "They aren't going to care about motive. The prosecutor will show that you are a drug user and that you had sex with the girl that afternoon. That will be enough. So we need to work around that."

He was right. Drugs and sex equaled motive even if it didn't add up to anything logical. I was not heavy into any drug. I smoked some. Who didn't? I tried a few things, thanks to Miranda and her friends.

Hawker played it wrong. He cleaned me up. He made me wear a suit and tie. He told me what to say when asked the hard questions. Worst of all, I think he believed I was guilty. Oh, he still wanted to win the case. He wanted me to go free. But he *believed* I was guilty. And I think that somehow came across to the jury, although I can't prove it. Afterwards, he tried calling for a mistrial but one was not granted.

And I had a judge who was trying to right some of the wrongs of the past. This young offender, perpetrator of such heinous crimes. I would be a test case for the new legislation on young people who commit violent crimes. I would get an adult sentence and go to an adult prison.

The only "good news" on that front was that the Severton Correctional Institution (prison, please) had a new wing reserved for violent offenders who were under twenty–one. And I'd have my own cell.

My father had to take out a second mortgage on the house. Hawker wasn't cheap even when he lost. The bill itself would probably not be fully paid off in my parents' lifetime. "Justice don't come cheap," were the words my lawyer used when discussing financial particulars with my parents.

At Severton, I expected… well, you can paint all the pictures for yourself. I don't need to spell them out here. But I was a "test case" and the youngest offender in the ward. So people were watching out for me. One of the guards, Eduardo, was assigned responsibility for me. "I'm going to see that you are treated fairly," he said. "Just don't ever, ever spit in my face." My reputation had preceded me. I promised Eduardo I would treat him with respect. And did. And he returned the favor by doing his job–which was to ensure my safety.

Other inmates intimidated me. They threatened me, said things that made my skin crawl. It wasn't like a weekend in Disneyworld or anything. It wasn't like a vacation behind bars. It was still a private hell in a locked room. I survived it. That's what I'll say about it. It could have been worse. But one day the door opened.

My long walk made the calves of my legs ache. And that felt good. It made my lungs work and that felt good too, but the mere act of breathing made me worry about Phyllis. Would she need an oxygen bottle for the rest of her life? Is that what smoking did to her? And I kept looking up at the empty branches of the trees around me. I wanted to see leaves on them again. While I was in Severton, I dreamed about green leaves on trees all the time. I dreamed about summer. I daydreamed about being with Lisa. I pretended she would still be there when I got out. I did this over and over to help keep it together. I still loved her. I deluded myself into thinking that she would be there. Even as I walked that day, looking up into the light filtering through the trees, I started to slip into that fantasy world where no one had been murdered. And that's when I realized I had taken a wrong turn. I wasn't on the bus route to my house anymore. I was headed to the outskirts of town. I'd gone east down Vogler Street. I was about a block from Lisa's home.

Chapter 10

I stared at the house for a long time. I looked at the backyard and beyond to the woods behind her house, where she and I had set up the tent and "camped." Ironically, I had always believed we were safe there. Hidden and away from the world. Free to do what we wanted. Sometimes we'd just lie on our backs and look up at the trees. Sometimes there were birds singing. Sometimes we were able to make the world go away.

Lisa was not like Miranda. Lisa had not had it all that easy. Heart problems as a child. An irregular heartbeat, lots of time sick, and missing school. And then an operation when she was thirteen. "I almost died," she said. "My heart stopped. I went… somewhere. It wasn't like on the TV shows. I couldn't see any light, no sound. I wasn't looking down on myself. I just felt like I was somewhere surrounded by people who cared for me. I don't remember anything else."

Lisa was all about causes. That's how she ended up in the demonstration that day. She wasn't a show–off angry protestor like I was. She almost didn't join. She was more a letter writer, a gentle persuader. That was her style. Convince one person at a time not to buy pencils from a factory that uses child labor, convince shoe buyers one at a time not to buy sweatshop running shoes–and you can change the world. That's what she believed. "You have to live what you believe in," was one of her favorite phrases. And she did.

She was hard at work convincing me to be a vegetarian. And failing.

She lectured me about AIDS orphans.

I think I was one of her causes–for a while at least. Not that she was a goody two–shoes who wanted to reform me. She liked that I was who I was. Let's call me rough around the edges.

She liked ice cream. She said she cheated a couple of times on school exams. She read books by Anaïs Nin and Henry Miller. She never watched television except for PBS nature shows. She liked coffee if it was "fair trade" and she'd grill whoever was selling a cup of it to find out where it came from and how the farmers were paid before she bought it.

Like me, she liked loud, offensive alternative music. She was opposed to all wars but thought that certain world leaders near and far should be assassinated. She wanted to save rainforests and ozone layers and arctic hares and minke whales and even lobsters. She wanted to stamp out racism and sexism and capitalism and several other "isms." Ironically, (if that is the right word here), she was in favor of capital punishment. And so were her parents. I'll let that settle in with you for a bit. The irony was not lost on me.

She claimed to be both a Christian and a pagan. "Have you decided what religion you want to be?" she asked sometimes. She thought that finding a religion was like shopping for a new pair of jeans. You look around until you find one you really like and try it on. Or you make a hybrid out of a couple of religions and call it your own.

Like her, I'd grown up going to a Protestant church. But I'd drifted away. During my trial (my many trials in the most Biblical sense), I had prayed again and always hoped for my prayers to be answered. They never were, up until the day of my release. Even then, it wasn't the thing that was number one on my list.

"You should read more," she said.

"I read too much already," was my lame answer.

"Not what they give you in school. You need to dig deeper."

Deeper was an odd word. She loaned me some of her Anaïs Nin books, which were mostly stories concerning sex. But she also loaned me books of poetry and politics and a book by Thomas Merton and one on palmistry.

"Let's go live on an island," she'd say. And she'd describe to me what it would be like there. "We'd grow our own food, build our own house, make our own clothes, and make love whenever we felt like it."

Lisa was a very sexual person and we would both go a little crazy sometimes.

For good or for bad, sex had a lot to do with us getting together. Adults are very confused about teenagers and sexuality. They know it is an emotional minefield but they offer advice that is near impossible to take. They would like you to curb your hormones but it's not just hormones. You feel the need to experience powerful emotions and that's part of the sex.

Now, don't get me wrong. I was never a find 'em and grind 'em kind of guy. I needed to feel an emotional connection. I was, or I believed I had been, in love with Miranda before Lisa came along. I had felt a very strong bond with her–and it was much more than the sex and the exotic danger of the drugs. I just wasn't ready to follow her in the direction she was going. I got out of that relationship to save *me*. Miranda seemed hell–bent on getting deeper into the drugs. I tried to get her to see how dangerous it could be. But she wouldn't listen. I should have stayed on her case. But after a while I gave up. And that was probably the biggest mistake of my life.

When Lisa first started showing an interest in me–and it was she who initiated our relationship–I was cool at first. She seemed too tame, too good. That was until our first date (if you could call it that) when she put her tongue down my throat and her hand on the crotch of my pants.

The tent in the woods behind her house was her idea. And I was the most willing of participants. I'll even admit that if it wasn't for the sex, I don't think I would have got to know the amazing and complex, wonderful and sometimes exasperating, but beautiful person that she was. Sex can take you far away from the mundane daily stuff of growing up and deliver you to that ultimate tropical island where two souls can mingle.

I used the word "souls" there. Lisa's word. Not mine. But I'd read enough of her books to believe that there must be something that is left after we die. And one of those books had said that sexual energy and spiritual energy were both part of the same thing.

"What same thing?" I had asked her–after making love, lying in that tent with the light filtered by the green nylon fabric.

"God," she said. "Everything that exists is God. It's all one thing."

I asked my lawyer, the not–so–clever Mr. Hawker, if there was any point during the trial when I could just speak freely about Lisa, about us. I'd told him some of the above in hopes that the story would reveal ultimately how much I loved Lisa.

Hawker stared at me and then said, "Let me get this straight. You want to go on the stand and talk about pagans and saving the freaking furry creatures, sex and God, and what else was it? Lobsters? You want to explain all *that* to a middle-aged jury made up of housewives and handymen?"

Needless to say I was told to say only the minimum. Hawker had a plan and his plan was to prove that the sex had been consensual and that the blood tests on me revealed that I only had traces of THC from the marijuana in my blood. And so did Lisa. (It was organic, supposedly. She had bought it from a friend. Farmers of the weed had been paid a fair trade price.)

But it still pretty much came down to drugs and sex by the time the prosecutor finished with me. And he had buried the idea of motive. We got high. I got carried away and killed her. That was what they wanted to believe.

I didn't just stand there all afternoon staring at Lisa's house. I knew it was a bad place for me to be. One part of me wanted to confront her mother, her father, and her sister and say to them how sorry I was about what happened. I'd never been given the opportunity. Despite Miranda's confession, I doubted that they were ready to be anything but hostile towards me.

It looked like such a normal suburban house. And hers, if ever there was one, was such a normal family. Her parents would try to figure out where Lisa had gone wrong. What had led her down this dangerous path? Was it something they did? Was it the weird books she read? Was it her hormones? Or would they just blame it all on me?

I walked back towards the main road and onward to where I'd catch the bus that would take me to my neighborhood.

"I'm sorry, Lisa," I said out loud. "I'm so sorry."

And my legs stopped working then. I crumpled and allowed myself to fall to my knees and put my hands over my face. I think I felt her presence then, or imagined it, because her face came back into my mind. I'd tried conjuring it so many times before in prison–but it would never come into focus and I'd have to take out her picture and look at it. Even then it seemed unreal, not like her.

Now I could see her if I kept my eyes closed. But it hurt so bad that I felt a pain in my chest. When I opened my eyes, there was a boy on a tricycle. He had ridden to the end of his driveway and now he was headed my way. I heard a door to the house open and a woman shout out to him. Then I realized she was running this way.

I started to get up, but felt unsure on my feet. I began to walk on slowly and I guess I was walking towards this woman's son. I'll never be sure if she recognized who I was but I won't forget the look in her eyes as she grabbed her little boy and then stared at me. She said nothing. She didn't have to.

Chapter 11

TV and newspaper reporters phoned the house and my mother told them I wasn't going to speak to them. "He's trying to return to a normal life," she said, but I didn't think that could ever happen. I spent a lot of time in my room. Prison had allowed me to adjust to being by myself. I could read for hours. It gave me that. I had trained myself to read any book I could get my hands on.

Lisa had been the one to teach me about leaping. "Pick a book that seems like the least likely book you'd want to read and give it a try. Just make the leap." She had loaned me several of her "leapers." Before I lost her, I had been reading Dostoevsky. Imagine. Me reading old dead Russian writers. She started me with *Notes from Underground*. And it was *Crime and Punishment* I was reading after that.

The pile of books in my bedroom were all from Lisa and Phyllis. *Pilgrim's Progress, Leaves of Grass, das Capital,*

The Art of War, Grapes of Wrath, Gulliver's Travels. Lisa had read all of them. Now it was my turn. I had many, many empty days to fill. My parents were worried about me. And I felt guilty about that. A son ruins his family's life. Then what? I was glad I did not have any brothers or sisters. Imagine what it would be like to have a brother who everyone believes is a murderer.

It's funny what went through my head during the following week. My parents tried to get me to do things–go for walks with them, go to movies, watch sports on TV, go for a family trip. I wasn't interested in any of it.

I thought about Lisa all the time. I ached for her. I felt total confusion when it came to Miranda. By now she was locked up. Unlike me, they did not treat her as an adult offender. She was in an all-girls correctional "facility"–Woodvale. I'd heard about the place. The inmates were allowed to live in cottages. You were locked into Woodvale, but you got to live in cottages. Even the murderers.

I couldn't begin to understand why Miranda had killed Lisa. All I knew was that it had something to do with me. Lisa and Miranda barely knew each other. I was the link. I was the reason. I knew that drugs were part of it. I knew how crystal meth could mess you up good. Lack of sleep. Paranoia. Feeling powerful and feeling scared. But it was more than the drugs. I could speculate–and I did way too much of that–but I had a craving, a need to know. Why?

I hated Miranda, I knew that. I hoped she'd stay locked away for a long, long time. But it wasn't just hate. I had this feeling that my own fate was somehow tied to hers. The story was not over. This haunted me late into the night–those terrible, dark nights when I could not get to sleep. My own sleeplessness had begun in Severton and followed me home to my own bedroom. The worst of it was imagining Lisa being stabbed, imagining what was going through her mind as she was dying.

In those golden moments when I could pull myself back from the brink of my own despair, here's what I thought about. I made a list of possibilities. The options went like this:

1. Get fat. Just take up eating as a serious pursuit. Food was an easy escape. Just go for it.

2. Go far away. With this one, often pondered in noble moments to save everyone a lot of grief, the question was always, how far and where to and what exactly would I do when I got there?
3. Return to school one day and pretend that nothing happened. Ignore the looks. Be a good student. Do my homework. Make new friends. (This was fantasy territory and much harder to envision than 1 and 2.)
4. Get back at someone or some thing. Revenge, pure and simple. Who exactly was I angry at? I had a list. The jury members. The judge. My idiot attorney – "the best in the business." Society. (Of course, but such a large task.) All those who believed I was guilty and treated me to their hatred. Or me. Just get back at me somehow for being such a screwup. This latter item seemed most satisfying.

And then, after dipping into the *I Ching* book or reflecting on something I'd read by Thomas Merton, I'd think of another option.

5. Prove to the world that I am a good person through doing great deeds. Like saving people or animals or rainforests or whales. As Lisa would want me to do.

It's when I thought of option 5 that I began to see the impossibility of my life. "Human wreckage" was the phrase I saw in the Dostoevsky novel. I was not the first or the last but a member of the tribe of human wrecks. Perhaps there was nothing for us but to litter the landscape of history, and age gracelessly into adulthood. And if that was going to be the case, I could settle in if I had one good and simple pleasure. Food might be enough. I'd eat well, get fat, and people would understand. They would say, "Look what happened to Michael Grove. He was smart, he showed promise. He went bad. He got blamed and then exonerated. But it ruined him. So he stayed home, became a burden to his family, and got fat. Isn't it a pity?"

Yes, that's what I wanted. I wanted pity. I wanted people to feel sorry for me. I didn't want to fix anything. And I couldn't change the past. So what could I do to bring on the pity? It was the path of least resistance.

I can imagine what you might think about this whole self–pity plan but I'd be lying if I told you that it didn't make me feel a little bit better. I'd never really pondered fat as a solution to one's problems. Now it seemed perfectly logical. I even started another list: hot dogs (the big, bloated, meaty ones infested with nitrates), ice cream (vanilla fudge), pizza (double pepperoni), cheese (I could develop an appetite for all kinds of cheese but I'd settle for Cheez Whiz if I had to), French fries (I could assume the title of King of the Transfats). This list could grow.

I could end up like one of those guys who has to be hauled out of the bathtub by unlucky firemen. I could be like that.

A week had gone by since my release. My parents were out. It was three in the afternoon. I was snacking in the kitchen. Cheez Whiz on celery. My mother's compromise. "If you are going to eat garbage, you should eat something healthy at the same time." Clog and unclog your arteries, was the way I translated that.

The doorbell rang.

I'd become good at not answering doorbells or phone calls.

It rang again. And again.

I saw an Acura parked in the driveway and didn't know anyone of my parents' friends who drove an Acura. Through the peephole in the door, I saw it was Josh Hawker. Good reason not to answer.

I think Josh knew I was home. Hell, where else would I be?

I opened the door. The fool was smiling. I blinked at the daylight and realized I had not set foot out of the house since I had visited Phyllis. I think part of me had believed the world had gone away or that it at least had decided that I was not part of it.

"Hi, Michael. Good to see you."

"Screw you too, Mr. Hawker," I said flatly.

"Good," he said. "Anger is good. We can work with that."

"Work on what?"

"Can I come in?"

"No."

He did not take this as an insult. He smiled. "We can use your anger to fuel our case."

"What case?"

"Wrongful conviction. What you've been through... this miscarriage of justice. You deserve compensation."

Compensation sounded like such a funny word. I couldn't help but laugh.

"You have been injured," he explained. "We can assign blame and demand compensation. That's the way it works."

"You think any of that can be repaired?" I asked sarcastically.

"No. But you can be compensated."

"How?"

"Money," he said. "Lots of it." He handed me a manila envelope. "I had my secretary put together a little package. Here are some news stories of other people wrongfully convicted who sued for compensation from the government. You were not the first."

"So now I'm part of some club of losers. And I should profit from my misery, everyone's misery? No way. What about Lisa's parents? What kind of compensation are they eligible for?"

"If they wanted to, they could make a case against that girl's family," he said matter-of-factly.

"Jesus," I said. "Does it all boil down to money?"

Hawker looked straight at me. "Michael, what else is there? I mean really. How else can you compensate someone for what you've been through? Rewire your brain, erase the memories, the punishment? Can't be done. So it's imperfect but it's something. Can I talk this over with your parents?"

"I thought I was deemed to be an adult. I thought I committed an adult crime, deserved an adult sentence. I thought the judge redrew the boundary of childhood just to make sure I was fully responsible."

"Something like that," Hawker admitted. "Take a look at the file. I'll call back. I never gave up on you, remember?"

"You were being paid, asshole," I said. "That's why you didn't give up on me."

He turned and started for his car. "Just take a look at the news clippings. I'm really hoping we can work together again."

I stood there blinking in the light. He hit the car remote and the car horn bleeped and the doors unlocked. "Wait a minute," I yelled to him. He took a few steps back in my direction.

"What did you really believe back then? I know you defended me. It was your job. But did you think I really did it?"

He looked up at the sky for a minute, trying to figure out how to answer this. He knew that his request depended on how he answered. And he must have opted for telling the truth. "Yes," he said. "I believed you did it."

I felt myself beginning to tremble with anger. But I was glad he said what he did. I knew it back then. I knew he never truly believed me.

"But now I'm giving you a way to get on with your life," Hawker said. "Think about it."

Chapter 12

There was a tent in the forest behind Lisa's house. We went there sometimes in the afternoons or evenings. While other kids were hanging out downtown on the street or in the malls, we escaped to this, our perfect little world. I thought it was the safest place on earth.

The tent belonged to Lisa's parents and they didn't seem to mind that we were alone back there. They didn't exactly like me, I could tell. But they had tremendous trust in their daughter. They knew she was smart and, in her own way, responsible. I think that they understood we were having sex. I really do. Lisa's mother had talked to her about AIDS and venereal diseases and had taken her to the doctor to get birth control.

I was the first guy she'd had sex with. She was not my first. Miranda was. But I had certainly not been Miranda's first partner.

I'm writing this to put in order the sequence of

things that happened. Unanswered questions haunt us for a long time. I am deeply haunted by many. But some things have been put to rest. I just want to say how it happened. I don't have all the answers as to why. But I've been working on that ever since Lisa's death.

Just so you don't think it was all about sex, let me say this. Lisa and I were very much in love. She and I were very different. She wanted to save the world. I wanted... what? Not to destroy it? Maybe just thumb my nose at it. Maybe write graffiti on it. It's easy to be young and angry even if you don't have a personal legitimate reason to be so. Miranda fed my anger and, at first, that was a kind of flattery. But I wanted to move on. And I thought she did too.

In our tent in the woods, Lisa and I sometimes just read. Yes. We sat quietly together with mosquitoes humming outside the confines of our screened windows and we read. Sometimes we'd read passages out loud to each other. There was philosophy and poetry and books on the environment. And novels. This all came up in the trial. *What were you doing that afternoon there in the woods?*

Imagine how it sounded to the jury. *We were reading.*

Of course that isn't the whole story. Sometimes we

just talked. Sometimes we listened to music. Sometimes we'd toke a little. Nothing more. Nothing less.

And sometimes we'd make love. Once or several times.

That was what the jury wanted to hear.

My lawyer, Mr. Hawker, kept referring to it as "consensual sex." The prosecutor kept referring to the events as simply sex and murder. Or when he chose to entirely ignore the truth, he used the word "rape." "She was murdered after all. After the sex. If it was 'consensual sex' why would this young man have murdered her?"

Why?

But he didn't murder her.

Nothing about Miranda ever came up in the hearing. Nothing.

We had made love twice that afternoon. I had to say this out loud.

Hawker thought the jury would understand. *Making love with your steady girlfriend two times in one afternoon cannot constitute rape. It was something they both agreed to.*

I understood even then, at sixteen, that sex was a powerful, emotional thing. It was a pleasurable thing and it was a dangerous thing. But if two people were in love, what was to hold them back?

With Miranda, it had always been a little bit strange, a little bit dark. She asked me to do things. She initiated it most times. I liked that at first. But the drugs made it confusing too. She was often higher than I was. The amphetamines and the meth, that was when it just got too weird. And all I could do was find the door, find my way out of that relationship. At first, she latched onto another guy and pretended she didn't care. Then there were a couple of nasty phone calls late at night.

And a scene at school. In the hallway. "You asshole," she said. "You gutless piece of shit. Why did I waste my time with you?"

This, because I stopped returning her phone calls. Stopped hanging out with her. Stopped trying to get her to clean up her act a little. "You have to draw a line somewhere," I lectured her. "I don't care if you want to get high for the rest of your life. But you have to decide when to back off. You have to recognize when something is starting to take over."

Like I was the big expert. I wasn't. I experimented with all kinds of shit but something in me kept backing me off. Mostly it was just the weed. Not that I think it's good for you or anything idiotic like that. I just believed I could handle it. Maybe that's what we all say.

Until it's too late.

If I were to make a list of the things that were most important to me back then I would have had Lisa at the top of the list. Drugs would have been on the list but not in the top ten. Getting high was a way of getting away from what I didn't like about school and the world around me. Being with Lisa was what I liked most about being alive. God or someone had given me a chance to spend time with someone that wonderful. Smart, beautiful, sexy, and loving. The anger was starting to boil off. The alienation was beginning to fade like an old pair of jeans.

Lisa was saving me from myself. And I can only wish she'd stayed around to finish the job.

That afternoon in the tent, we made love twice. Sexy, wonderful, beautiful. I had no idea that someone was nearby watching.

I'd promised my parents I'd be home for dinner at five p.m. My aunt and uncle were coming over. I didn't do a lot of things my parents asked, but I liked Ruth and Charlie.

I had lived with them one summer when I was younger at a time when my parents were having problems. I hadn't seen them for a long while. *Sure, I'd be home by five.*

Lisa and I had both fallen asleep in the tent. I woke and checked my watch. "Gotta go," I said. "I'll walk you back to your house."

"No," she said, "I'm still sleepy. I like it here. I'm going to sleep a little more and then go in."

The forest was just beyond Lisa's backyard. It was a shelter and a familiar place to us, a place of great privacy. We always felt safe there.

"Okay," I said. "You got your cell phone?"

"Yes. But it's off of course."

"Turn it on. I'll call you after I get home."

"A wake–up call?"

"Yes."

But I never called. Ruth and Charlie were already at my house. They were in good spirits and wanted to talk. I guess I figured I'd call Lisa at home after they left.

The police phoned my house at nine o'clock that evening. My aunt and uncle were still there. My life as I knew it ended with that phone call. The storyline that was my life made a certain amount of sense up until then. Then the nightmare began.

When I was released, some people used the phrase that I could "pick up my life where I left off." But those words were hollow. It could not possibly work that way. One thing was shattered. Another thing began. What was needed was a new beginning. But that would not be easy.

I thumbed through Hawker's package of clippings about wrongful convictions and was shocked at how many there were. Supposed murderers spending years or even decades in prison and then released after new DNA testing or after confessions or new evidence. Suits were filed by the wrongfully convicted. Thousands of dollars, hundreds of thousands of dollars. In some cases over a million. Hawker was hoping I'd get greedy, hoping I'd want revenge on the system. Hoping he could get a big piece of the action.

I went a bit further–perverse interest now. I was part of some unlucky elite: murderers who were suddenly no longer murderers and set free. I searched their names on the Internet and tried to find out what happened after the poor sods were set free and sued for damages. Did the money make for happiness?

The sad truth was that I could not find a single instance of truly renewed lives. The longer the sentence, the worse the damage. I was the poster child of the club. Only sixteen and free before his seventeenth birthday. But it didn't feel like that.

Along my search, I stumbled on old news stories of my own trial. The papers had painted me as a monster. I doubted I could shed that image now that it was so deeply implanted in the mind of the public.

Chapter 13

I woke up in the morning thinking about capital punishment. In prison, I'd read some articles about the pros and cons of it. There had been an essay by the French writer, Albert Camus, "Reflections on the Guillotine." And another author who argued that someone wrongfully convicted of a murder and put in prison is so damaged by it all that it would be more humane had he been put to death instead. It scared the hell out of me to be reading the stuff while inside. But I'd read it anyway.

I'd been home for ten days. Mostly hibernating. There was the school issue. My parents had met with the principal. They had a dream. I would return to classes, catch up on some work, graduate with my class from high school–conditional upon taking some summer classes.

As if nothing had happened.

In English class once prior to the murder, Mr. Gelbert made us each take part in a debate. One on one.

I was up against Lisa on the issue of capital punishment. This was back before we were very close. I knew who she was. She knew who I was. That was about it.

She was for. I was against. I know, it seems odd. Lisa, the great humanitarian, wanting the death penalty. We had both done research, although I could see that Lisa was much sharper at this sort of thing than me. And passionate. She probably believed in what she was arguing. I was just kind of wishy–washy, didn't really feel that strongly one way or the other, but I took this topic because I thought it would be easy.

I based part of my argument on the fact that the legal system was flawed and always would be. You might end up convicting the wrong person and ending his or her life. And besides, capital punishment is not a deterrent.

Lisa had agreed. It was not a deterrent. People who murdered were not thinking about the consequences. But I can still remember her rebuttal. "Sadly," she said, "I argue that capital punishment is still the best option, despite my opponent's worthy points. Even if it is a wrongful conviction. It is the most humane option."

I was a little stunned by what she had said, didn't

know how I would finish my rebuttal now that she had thrown this in. But it seemed like absurd logic.

"My point is this," Lisa said with conviction. "Most imprisonment damages the life of the convicted in such a powerful and corrupting way that one can never return to normal. The loss of freedom, the deterioration of the spirit, and the disruption of a life through imprisonment is worse than death. The harm is irreparable. Thus, assuming that the right criminal is convicted most of the time, it is better to endorse capital punishment rather than any alternative."

She had cited several sources. She was not alone in her thinking. But it totally threw me off.

Mr. Gelbert cleared his throat. "Michael, now for your closing words."

I remember looking at Lisa and she suddenly seemed concerned for me. She realized she had thrown me off with her final argument. "I don't know," I said, looking down at my notes. "I... um... still think it's wrong to kill someone. Even if they murdered. I'm sure they can be rehabilitated. Somehow." I leafed through my notes but couldn't find anything else to say that I hadn't already said. I think I shrugged then and said something like, "Aw, hell. Lisa's probably right. How the hell are you gonna fit back into society if your life's been ripped out from under you?"

A brilliant way to end a debate on my part, I thought. The class laughed and Mr. Gelbert said, "That will be all. Please step down."

The next debate was over legal prostitution, pro and con.

As Lisa and I walked out of class that day, she said, "Sorry," in a soft voice as she walked past me, not giving me eye contact. I thought she was cute, sure. I thought a lot of girls were cute. And as she walked away, I noticed her hair. I should have told her I really liked her hair. But I didn't. She wasn't exactly on my radar then. A good student. I think she was on student council. I think she helped raise money for AIDS orphans in Africa. She was that kind of girl. I know she got an A on the debate. I received a lowly C, which was probably more than I deserved.

And now, waking up, ten days into freedom, I was thinking about that debate, realizing she was right. I'd only been incarcerated for six months and I was certain my life was ruined forever. Lisa had been right. The damage was done. It was irreparable. I didn't really want to live like this. Screw rehabilitation. It wasn't going to happen.

I was having a hard time getting out of bed in the mornings. I was depressed. Go figure. My brain locked onto weird shit. Like this capital punishment thing. And then this.

A scene. Something like a movie. I'm in a room. My wrists are tied. A doctor with rimless, round lens glasses is about to administer a lethal injection. There is an audience behind the glass. Lisa's parents. My parents. And in the scene, a bunch of kids from school. They are chewing gum and pointing at me. I nod in their direction. And then I feel the needle. And I go cold.

It all seems so easy. Not at all like what I was going through.

I went downstairs for breakfast. The clock said 11:45 but the time on clocks didn't mean that much to me any more. It must have been a Saturday because both my parents were home.

"Mr. Hawker phoned again," my dad said. "What do you think?"

"What do *you* think?" I asked.

"I don't know. Your mother and I think something needs to be done."

"Something?"

"It's not the money," he said. "It can't be about the money."

"Well, you lost your job. Whose fault was that?" I asked.

"I know."

"Maybe you should do something. I just don't think I want any part of what Hawker is proposing."

My mother came in the room then. "Your aunt and uncle think you should do a TV interview. They know someone who would do a good job. We could do it here. We'd have a say on how it was edited. Clear the air once and for all."

I shook my head. "I'd screw it up," I said. "I don't think I could do it, anyway. Look at what the media already did. They don't care if it's truth or lies, as long as it's a good story. What the media does well is generate hate and mistrust," I said and then felt a shudder go through me. Those final words were Lisa's, not mine. Those were her exact words. She never watched TV.

She didn't trust the news.

"There's got to be something," my mother said.

I sat there glumly. The boy beyond repair, that was my story. *Well, Oprah, it really kind of sucked losing my girlfriend and ending up in the slammer. And having everyone think I raped and murdered her. But you get over these things. And the upside is: I lost ten pounds while in prison and improved my mind.* And then the audience would applaud and they'd cut to a commercial for Pampers.

My parents yammered about going for a car trip. A lake, a mountain, a beach. Nothing sounded appealing. "I think I'll just go back to bed."

"Don't you think you are sleeping too much?"

"That's what I learned to do in prison. I learned to sleep. It wasn't like sleeping here. It was different. I went away when I slept. And I was always, always shocked when I woke up again and realized the bad stuff wasn't just a dream. Do you know what that's like?"

They both sat silently now. My pain was their pain. Another good reason for capital punishment. *Just make the bad boy go away so everyone else can start over.*

And so I slept some more.

I didn't know just then that I was waiting for something. I thought I was still waiting to be punished. For I still felt I deserved punishment. Lisa was dead. I was alive. I hated that trade–off.

And I did not want forgiveness. That's what I think my parents believed I needed. But I wasn't ready for it and wasn't sure I'd ever be ready for it.

It was nearly five in the afternoon, nearly dinner time. I'd slept through another day. I heard the phone ring. Someone answered it. My mother knocked on my door.

"Yeah?" I said.

"It's your grandmother. She wants to talk to you."

Phyllis. She was the only person I was willing to take a call from. I could never say no to her. I got out of bed and picked up my phone. I waited for my mother to hang up.

"Michael?"

"Yeah, Grandmom."

"I asked you not to call me that."

"Sorry, Phyllis. I'm just waking up."

"I know about the sleep thing, Michael. When your grandfather died I was working on the world's record."

"Is there a world's record for sleep?"

"Yes, but it's hard to beat the ones in comas. They can hang on for years before they wake up. Nothing like a good coma, I say, to keep the world off your back."

"You're nuts," I said with the first hint of a smile on my face in a long while. I heard something funny, a sucking of breath, "You're not smoking are you?"

"Jesus. Can't get away with anything. Don't worry. These are lettuce cigarettes. Bought them at the health food store." There was another sucking of air and something that sounded like bubbles in water.

"But your lungs. Anything with smoke could hurt you."

"I know. That's why I bought this hookah thing–like a bong but something they use in the Middle East for tobacco. The water cools the smoke. You should try it."

"Save me some of your lettuce cigarettes. I'd love to try them."

"They come in menthol, too. Although I prefer the regulars. No nicotine, though. So I chew the gum and wear the patch. It's still not the same."

"And?"

"And what?"

"Why did you call?"

"Because I did the *I Ching* for you. Threw the sticks. And guess what?"

"What?"

"Hexagram 33."

"Let me guess. Something to do with inner strength. Wings like eagles. Eyes like hawks."

"No way. Hexagram 33 can be interpreted this way: *Once you decide to retreat from the world, do it with determination. If you act with full regret you will not be successful.* That's why I thought I should call you right away. Do you understand what the sticks are saying?"

Coming from anyone else but her, I would have thought it the flakiest thing in the world. But it triggered some miniscule connection in my brain. She was saying what no one else had said to me yet. She was giving me permission.

Permission to be alone with my suffering. Permission to hide from the world for as long as I wanted.

And that was the first time I felt some relief from all the weight on my shoulders. I think that was the first full breath of air I took in my lungs since I got the phone call that night.

Chapter 14

Unless you've had significant first–hand experience with tragedy in your life at sixteen, you truly know nothing of death. In North America, it is a thing on the news daily but it is a form of entertainment–the stories about accidents and murders and natural disasters. My grandfather had died when I was young and that had startled me and upset me, of course. But it was amazing how quickly I moved on to whatever was of interest to me then–baseball or bicycles or studying paperbacks about performing magic tricks.

Prison allowed me to read widely about death. Reading was this gift that Lisa had given me. Sure, I knew how to read but she had a passion for it. She was already well beyond anything our teachers were teaching us. When it came to reading, she consumed everything. Her words, not mine. But they fit. She'd sample broadly from any book in the library she could get her hands on.

She believed in books. I can almost say it was her religion. My word, not hers.

The prison library was not great but not bad. We could request books through the public library system, though, so if one was patient, all the world's literature was available. When I read, I felt close to Lisa again. And I read quite a bit about what happens after you die.

I know every kid thinks about this. But I rarely considered it. It was almost like I didn't want to waste my time on something I could do nothing about. *When you die, I guess you figure out what death is all about.* I was all about living. Not that I loved everything about life. Much of it sucked. But I was the here–and–now sort. Eat, drink, and be cynical. For tomorrow…

I begged for a ghostly apparition of Lisa in my book-strewn cell. Yes, I read books, serious books, on ghosts. On communication with the dead. But I fell short of trying to call her back somehow. I almost thought it actually was possible, but what if she appeared and saw me in Severton? What would she think? Would this hurt her in some way? I read about angels. Lots of books about angels. So many first-hand experiences. Were they all making it up? Could it be possible that it was all bullshit? Or was there truth here?

If there be angels, then one, Lisa perhaps, watched over me in Severton. Eduardo, however, was my on-the-ground "angel." I was, after all, a test case. He had the responsibility of preventing the headline: *Young murderer murdered in Severton*. I had my private cell, my "unit," as it was called. I had my books to protect me and I think I had–or liked to think I had–an angel watching over me. Lisa.

How I longed to feel her touch me. And how often I was haunted by the very last physical contact we had. Just before she fell asleep in the tent, just before I left, I kissed her. Our lips held together, then parted. I touched her face. And left.

Those few seconds exist somewhere out of time, I believe. They exist in the present and in the past and in the future. The universe began with an explosion, expanded, collapsed, and returned to a dot of pure compact everything and nothing. But all the while that kiss remains.

Like I say, I read a lot. It wasn't like I was killing time or trying to do something "useful." Every word I read was Lisa. Every page turned was Lisa. That's how good it was–the reading. And that's how bad it was–the pain of missing her.

Inside, I became many things. I was already a cynic. Now I was a more sophisticated one. I was a misanthrope. I shed years of youth–there would be nothing left of the boy by the time my verdict was overturned. The boy had fled. He'd been bullied away. I also became an intellectual. Lisa and books and my library card. There was beauty still in ideas. In concepts. In stories. In the way language shaped itself on the page. Eduardo said, "Michael, you read so many books. You yourself should become a writer. Tell your story in print."

"Do you believe I'm innocent?" I asked him more than once.

"I believe that you believe you are innocent. What I believe does not matter. I believe that if you write a book and it sells, you may get out sooner. You may remember that I was fair to you. Maybe you'd make a lot of money and buy me an in–ground swimming pool." It was an odd thing to say.

"That's all you want? An in–ground swimming pool?"

"Yes," he said. "I think I'd be happy and so would my wife and kids."

As you can imagine, I read law books. And books on psychology. I was never denied a single request. I was allowed to read a book on devil worship by a scholar of the occult. I was permitted books on human sexuality. I read several sacred texts from Hinduism and Buddhism. I read Malcolm X's *Autobiography* and that inspired me for a while. Every inmate of every prison should be required to read this.

I understand how far–fetched this sounds. I would never have done this if I had not been locked up. This is not to say that I completely loved books. I loathed life at that point and therefore everything included in that category. But books were a matter of survival. John Fowles, Ken Kesey, R.D. Laing, Bertrand Russell, books on social justice. Outdated or contemporary. I even read the *Kinsey Report*. And after that, Kubler–Ross and her books about death and dying. Near death experiences. So similar and universal in all cultures though some scientists conclude that it is not real. You are not traveling to the next dimension through that tunnel with light at the end. It is simply a hallucination brought on by hypoxia, an inadequate supply of oxygen in the brain.

When I read that last bit, I fell into a kind of despair. Everything can be explained through science. You believe you are going some place beautiful and it is just the lack of oxygen in your brain.

And then you die.

This option presented itself to me over and over. No purpose, no plan, no real before or after existence of the mythical soul. *When you die, you die.* I had friends in high school who told me they believed this. A couple of my fellow inmates in prison expressed this view. Basic. Matter–of–fact. The lungs stop functioning. The heart stops. Make room on the planet for another bag of skin to pretend it all has meaning.

They let me read books about suicide and suicide prevention. I thought that was brave of the librarian–a rather old, thin man, bald with the boniest of skulls. The others called him Mr. Bones but I never did. He took his job seriously. Ordered me books from the public library and had them sent here by courier. When I asked him why he worked here, he answered, "For the pension. I'll be out of here in five years and I'll have a good pension." But I think it was more than that. I could tell by the way he reacted to my requests.

I meant to test him one day. Ask for a book on some aspect of terrorism or one on home manufacture of drugs. But I decided not to push it. A good thing is a good thing when you are incarcerated. You didn't want to mess with that. So the suicide books were about the limit. Oh, my "counselor" in Severton heard pretty quick about that. I suppose Mr. Bones was worried about more than his pension. I think he had a good heart.

Mr. Bones, when he had seen me reading Dostoevsky early on, thought I was faking. "I've seen this game before," he said, but there was no real accusation in his voice.

"What game?" I said.

"The model prisoner."

"They all read the Russians?"

"Some. Why Dostoevsky?"

His question made me think of Lisa. It was her suggestion. My eyes began to tear. "It was recommended," I said. "Different time, different place."

"You ever read Tolstoy?"

"He's on my list," I said. The truth was I wanted to move on from the dark Russian novelists. Not exactly the thing to sustain you inside.

Mr. Bones handed me a big fat book that I expected to be *War and Peace* but turned out to be *Anna Karenina.* "Yikes," I said.

"Yikes is right," was all Bones said. "May not be your cup of tea." He began to take the book back.

"No. I'll give it a try. Model prisoner game, remember?"

It was rough sledding, I admit, but the passages about death and dying drew me in. In one scene, a girl is contemplating suicide by throwing herself under a freight train. She has been hurt. She wants to punish the man who hurt her and she wants to punish herself. She throws herself in the path of the oncoming train and then has second thoughts.

The author wrote: *And just at that moment she was horror-struck by what she was doing. Where am I? What am I doing? She tried to get up, to remove herself but some monstrous thing struck her on the head and dragged her down. "Lord forgive me for everything," she murmured, and knew there was no point in struggling.*

No happy endings for the Russians. Later, I would turn to those psychology books on suicide and learn that men were more successful at it than women and they preferred violent means to an effective end. Men, I suppose, like to get the job done. Women like to change their mind along the way. The shrinks had two categories: "attempters" and "completers." Guys, you know which team you're on. Pills were for girls, guns for guys. Hot baths and slit wrists for the ladies, a good leap from a tall building and a splat for the gents.

Dr. Kaufman had once asked me some questions that were supposed to determine if I was headed down this path and rightfully concluded I was not. Guess he got one thing right.

I learned about the myths surrounding suicide. People who talk about it rarely do it. Not true. *People who do it are definite death is for them.* Apparently, like the girl in Anna K, most people think life still seems like an option when sucking a barrel of a gun. *Suicide is the result of depression.* Sometimes yes, sometimes no. Could just be that TV keeps getting worse and worse. Nothing more, nothing less. *Folks who commit suicide are crazy.* This would be a personal favorite. Many people who are crazy–let's call this "out of touch with reality"–are corporation CEOs and presidents. The rest of us only wish there was a connection. And then some people think it has to do with *sun spots, phases of the moon, or the position of planets in the solar system*. A good solar flare could get you down and it is a bummer when Jupiter is hiding behind Mars. But for most, a six–pack of beer or a good toke would get you past that.

Two main motivators, however, the real things that make people want to do it and, for some, actually do it are these. Numero uno. *You want out; you want it all to stop, to go away. And number two. You want to manipulate the world; that is, you want revenge, you want to hurt or you want someone to recognize, after your death, the way it really was.*

I had both of those feelings many times after Lisa's death. I continued to have them in my own dark days after my release. Up until the time Phyllis called me and gave me permission to hide out from the world, to retreat, I wanted out and I wanted revenge.

But I'd not even moved anywhere near the "attempter" category, let alone join the masculine "completer" camp. Reasons? I couldn't do it to my parents. To Phyllis. And the gnawing, stomach churning feeling that I was *supposed* to do something. There was something that Lisa would have wanted me to do.

I just didn't have a clue as to what that something was.

Chapter 15

No. My suicide riff was not a cry for help. Humanity's cry for help began with the first words ever uttered. We want someone or something to save us. We want to be protected. We want to be in a safe place. And we want to be loved. Even now, these five years later, even now, knowing what I know, this is all I want. If you are like me, you have already realized these things are unachievable. You are born, you suffer, and you die.

But somewhere in there, you want one great thing to happen. You want something of significance. You want it all to *mean* something.

So after another two days of my "retreat," of my parents' furtive hallway–whispering of their worries about my mental health, my depression and my despair, I woke up and it was raining. Raining hard.

And all I could think about was getting the hell out

of the house.

I walked downstairs and ate cornflakes at eight a.m. I checked my messages. Hawker had called. *Screw him.* Kaufman had called. *Ditto.* Mr. Tyson, my principal, had called and spoken with my parents about a "reintegration plan." At least he had the stones to call my parents. After what he'd said about me to the media. "Not yet," I said. "I'm not ready yet."

"But if you want to graduate ..." my mom began. She looked so sad. And I felt sorry for her. She wanted it all to be like normal. Her son graduating from high school. Like everybody else.

"These things take time," I said. Her own words for me so many times growing up. But I was being cruel.

"I know," she said.

"We just want what's best for you," my father added, a tired and familiar expression of his own hopelessness.

"I'm going out to walk around for a while."

"It's raining."

"I'll put on rain gear. You still have my coat?"

"Of course. We wouldn't throw anything away," my dad said. But as soon as he said it, it implied something that reminded us all of prison, of the possibility that I may not have ever needed my rain jacket again.

My mother produced jacket from the kitchen closet. Nothing had been sequestered away to the attic. Nothing.

"Where are you going?" my mom asked.

"I'm not sure. I just want to walk." I was standing now, trying to hide some small thrill coupled with a fear that I was actually about to go out again into the streets of my town on my own. Free and without restraints.

"Take the cell phone," my dad said. "Call us if you want me to pick you up or anything. Anything."

"Don't you have to go to work?"

"Not today," he said. And I didn't ask why. But I understood.

"See you guys later."

Sudsy was backing his car out of the driveway when I walked out into the slackening rain. His window was half rolled down and I caught that look again before he quickly rolled it back up.

After retreat, the *I Ching* may or may not have said–since I'm making this up–*after retreat, one waits for the elements to be favorable and then one ventures cautiously out into the light of day.* Or the damp gloom of a morning in the hometown, if need be.

I would be lying to you if I said that it did not feel good. The voices in my head were a dulled background conversation. Once Sudsy's Toyota had pulled away, there was no one watching me. With my raincoat hood up, no one recognizing me. The sidewalks were empty. Cars hissed by on the wet street.

I saw a school bus and I stopped dead in my tracks. It was my bus. My old bus. A couple of kids from the neighborhood were getting on. Pen Walker and Graeme. Nicole. Nicole who had once been a friend of Lisa's. I had a sudden impulse to run for the bus at the stop. Get on. Take a seat in the back and see what happened. Pen Walker, I think, would talk to me. But not Nicole or Graeme.

But it was too early. I remained frozen in my tracks. I was not yet part of the world. A world that had moved on. I was still an outsider. That's what had become so clear to me that day I had ventured out to see my grandmother. From then on, I would always be an outsider.

The door of the bus closed and it moved forward. The rain began to come down harder but I didn't mind. There was a strange metallic taste in my mouth and I wondered why. It was the taste of rainwater, I realized, trickling down my cheek into my mouth. It reminded me of summer. And Lisa. Lisa and I emerging from the tent in the woods on a rainy day. The taste of her in my mouth mingled with rainwater.

Suddenly I knew that everything that would happen to me day after day, possibly for the rest of my life, would remind me of her. Lisa's friend, Nicole. The rain. The bus. Pick anything. I had discovered that each memory of Lisa, no matter how fine, was followed by a feeling of panic. The panic I felt now. I would have to get over this. I would learn how to cope. Otherwise, I would not be able to go out into the world. I would curl up in my bed into a fetal position and stay that way forever.

The rain eased again, I walked on. I was tracing the public bus route to my grandmother's. I don't think I was really headed there. I just needed a path that was familiar. I put my hand around the cell phone in my pocket. If I really came unglued, if the panic set in and I could not put it at bay, I would call my father, who had taken off from work just in case his son needed him.

The orderliness of the front yards seemed like a

strange thing to me. Close–cropped grass, paved driveways, flowerbeds, trimmed hedges. I found it hard to imagine a life where these things took priority. A world full of pain and suffering and injustice, and a person still has time or money to keep the lawn well–trimmed? What an odd thing.

I was headed towards a busy part of town. Strip malls with convenience stores, dry cleaners, coffee shops.

Coffee. Suddenly I wanted a cup of coffee more than anything in the world. Not the pathetic Severton coffee–so weak and bitter it was almost like a tease, not anything worth even attempting. But the sadness of sitting alone in a coffee shop on a rainy morning seemed too great to bear.

I recognized the corner and remembered the black man who had talked to me on the bus. This is where he got off. Over there was where he worked. Mighty Man Muffler. I walked in that direction, went in, and heard a buzzer go off. It was the exact same sound as the buzzer that sounded whenever the door to my "unit" opened. A chill went down my spine.

A slick–haired white man behind the counter looked

at me. I pulled the hood down and tasted rainwater again, the taste of Lisa in my mouth. "What can I do for you?"

I looked at the tool calendars on the wall, the ones with scantily clad women with large breasts standing beside hot rods. Pictures from some other planet. "Louis," I said, remembering his name. "I wonder if I could speak to Louis."

"Sure," the counter man said. "I'll call him. You take a seat."

I sat by a bored man in a business suit who was watching CNN on a small waiting room TV. There was footage of a house fire with a woman in a window holding onto a baby. Then a story about a flood somewhere out west, then a hostage taking. Each item was thirty seconds long. TV for the short attention span. It occurred to me that the footage of me leaving the courthouse the day of my conviction had probably flashed on this and millions of other TV screens.

The bored man reacted to what he saw. "Those poor folks," he said. But I didn't know if he meant the lady with the baby, the flood victims, or the hostages. The camera lingered a few more seconds on the hostage takers–terrorists in muddy military garb caught on someone's video cell phone as they abducted a bank manager. "People like that don't deserve to live," the man said, looking at me, waiting for a response.

But I was thinking about me on that screen. He would have said the same thing. *Doesn't deserve to live.* Judgment would have been rendered by all the CNN viewers. Justice denied. Verdict delivered. Punishment instant. If they had their way. I said nothing and nodded.

Louis arrived in dirty overalls, wiping his hands on a rag. He looked at me for a second, said the same "What can I do for you?" But then paused.

I didn't really know what to say but "Hi, I was in the neighborhood."

Louis recognized me now. "Looks like you're on your way to go fishing," he said. And smiled.

I smiled back. "No. Just going for a coffee. Wondered if you could join me."

Louis kept wiping the grease off his hands, turned to the man at the counter. "What's the lineup look like?"

The slicked–back guy took a look at a clipboard. "Pretty well under control now. Gets busy around eleven.

If you're gonna take a break, now's the time."

"Smooth," Louis said and unzipped the overalls. Underneath he just had a flannel shirt and jeans. He grabbed a heavy raincoat from a rack. "I'll be over at the coffee shop if you need me."

We walked silently across the wet street, got two coffees and a pair of jelly–filled doughnuts, and sat down by the window.

"I'm glad you came," Louis said.

"I'm not sure why I did. This is a little weird."

"Tell me about it. 'Little weird' is putting it lightly. I knew almost right away who you were on the bus. My first instinct was to do you a favor and not stare like those others. Then I said to myself: Louis, you been there, or somewhere like it. What would you want? And what would Jesus do?"

"Jesus?" I was almost afraid he was going to get preachy. But he didn't.

"Oh, hell. Jesus or Martin Luther King or my old Uncle Arthur." He paused to sip coffee and take a bite of doughnut, allowing some of the jelly to squeeze out and fall onto the table. "Or Malcolm X."

"You read Malcolm X?"

"Of course I did. Anyone who goes inside and doesn't read Malcolm X is a fool."

"Severton?"

"Three years. Armed robbery. I was a fool but I read Malcolm X."

"Bones. Mr. Bones?"

"Who? Oh yeah, that's what they called him. Skullbones, I called him. I told him I hated books and he put Malcolm's book in my hand. That and the *Bible*. I read 'em both. My granddaddy had been telling me to read the damn *Bible* all my life. I kept saying I never had time. Well, sir, suddenly I didn't have any excuse."

"I was in six months," I said.

"I know. I read about you in the papers. You know what I thought the first time I read about you, during the trial?"

"I can imagine. You thought I was guilty."

"No. I *knew* you were guilty. Not that I trusted the courts. It's just that I saw you on TV. Read about you in the news. It was crystal clear. Spoiled young white boy who has too much of everything. Never learned an ounce of self–control. Has everything a guy could dream of and he destroys it and he destroys himself."

"And he deserves to die?"

"Maybe that's what I was thinking."

"And now?"

"Look, Michael–see, I even remember your name–Michael, I don't really know you at all. I just know a little of where you are *at*. I believe now you didn't do it but I could be wrong even about that. I just know some of what you went through."

"So why did I come here to talk to you?" I asked.

Louis asked. "You gotta talk to someone. I just gave you the option."

"Louis, were you guilty?"

"Damn straight. I tried to weasel out of it but they had me on video. I'd have lied and done anything. But there it was."

"Were you angry when you got out?"

"Yes. Even though I got what I deserved. I was angry about being caught."

"Doesn't sound all that noble."

"Noble? Not much noble about me. But all that time

inside was good for me–like some kind of bad tasting medicine your mother gives you when you're a kid."

"Do you think I'm supposed to feel something like that? Swallowed the awful medicine, learned a few lessons, now get on with it?"

"What, muffler repair? No, son. I don't know what you *take* from the experience. I just know where you've been and where you are at. More or less."

"But what the hell do I do?" My voice was a little too loud. I was confused as to why I came to Louis, someone I didn't know, and exactly what he was offering.

Louis took a big gulp of coffee, crammed the rest of his doughnut in his mouth and before he swallowed said, "Just what you're doing right now. Call it what you want. I call it reaching out. What you do next is up to you."

His voice was also a little too loud now. People were looking at us. But Louis was smiling. "Let 'em stare, son. You'll get used to it. My motto has always been, 'Don't let the bastards get you down.' C'mon, let's go. I gotta get back to work."

Chapter 16

School. Every time I thought about it, I started to sweat. I'd been home for three weeks. Winter was starting to fade and spring was on its way. My parents were low–key about everything. "Just get through the day, Michael," my mother would say. "The more distance you put behind you, the easier it will be." I guess I understood what she meant about distance. It's just that I still carried around so much hurt and loss.

I never actually came out and said no to Josh Hawker so he was persistent–though he was starting to take the hint. "The clock is ticking," he said to me on the phone. "The longer you let this go, the more difficult it may be for us to get a proper settlement." Proper settlement meant lots of money. And I thought about it sometimes. What would it be like to have a lot of money? Would I be happier? Would my parents? The answer seemed to be no. But I knew that my father was still paying off the legal bills from the trial. I just didn't have the guts to face up to any of it. Not with Hawker and not with a legal system that worked so badly.

But the clock was ticking on a lot of fronts. The principal's offer to try to reintegrate me and fast–track me to graduation (with the make–up summer courses to follow) wouldn't last forever. If I waited too long, the school year would be nearly over.

What exactly was I afraid of? *Don't let the bastards get you down.* The wisdom of Louis. Who exactly were the bastards he referred to, you might wonder. Or maybe you already know.

The bastards are the ones who want to see you hurting. They are the ones who believe they are better than you. The ones who hate to see you get a break or have good luck or a shot at anything good. Oh, I knew who the bastards were. Men and women. Boys and girls. Sudsy next door with his familiar glare through the car window. And some of the ones from school who had believed I got what I deserved. The ones who had sent me e–mails during my trial, the ones who had talked about me in chat rooms. They'd still be there in school, waiting for me to fall on my face or fail or screw up somehow.

And it was for them that I would return to school, I finally declared to myself. I wasn't going to let them win. If I could pull it off, they'd have to suffer through me walking up and receiving my high school diploma with them.

So this is how it went. I had been staying in my room for several days in a row. Reading *Heart of Darkness*, one of Skullbones' recommendations. "Skip the light stuff," he said. "I prefer the serious writers." He was referring to Conrad, Faulkner, Marquez. *A Hundred Years of Solitude.* Now there's a cheery title.

But it was on my third day of self–imposed reading isolation with the Conrad and Marquez *(Love in the Time of Cholera)* that the strange librarian's advice made something click in my head. It was almost like a vision. I could almost see the words presented in neon beyond the pool of the reading lamp light. It was that real. *What do you have to lose?*

"Nothing." I said it out loud.

I had nothing to lose. I had already lost it all. I was free.

Strangely enough, my parents almost tried to stop me. They thought I had lost my mind. "Why today?" my dad asked.

"What do I have to lose?" was my answer.

He looked me in the eyes and drew a deep breath. "I'll drive you. When do you want to go?"

"Now," I said.

"I'll call Mr. Tyson and tell him you're coming."

"Tell him I look forward to seeing him again."

My mother looked stunned.

Sudsy, predictably, was walking out to his car just as we emerged from the house. He scowled at us. Bastard number one. I took this as a good omen. Yes, I could do this. Bring 'em all on.

Mr. Tyson was remarkably cool about my arrival. Professional, I suppose, but down–to–earth.

"Michael, this isn't going to be easy."

"I know."

"Good. I put together a schedule for you that I think will work. Each of these teachers has indicated they want to help."

"I'd prefer I didn't get any special treatment."

"Right. It's just that some teachers said they'd be uncomfortable having you in the classroom. And, frankly, there are some teachers here I don't trust."

"Wow," I said, wondering why he offered up that bit of news. "Really?"

"Really. Don't ask me to name names. You know that the other students will be watching you. I don't know how you're going to handle that."

"I don't know either."

"Then I guess you play it by ear and see how it goes."

I wanted to say something sarcastic but didn't. I liked Tyson now, realized I never knew him at all. I had always thought he was an asshole. Now he had just earned himself membership in a small circle of people who I believed were on my side. And that circle was mighty small.

There was an awkward silence as we waited for the bell that indicated the end of first period. He handed me a piece of paper with my schedule printed on it. "Mr. Gelbert's English class, Room 314. You want me to walk you there?"

"No," I said. "I'd rather do this on my own."

"Brave man."

Gelbert had been coached, I could tell. He nodded when I walked in and pointed to a seat by the windows. I avoided eye contact, heard the murmurs, kept my own attention on Gelbert. He didn't say a word about me and acted as if I wasn't there. "Can someone tell me what an oxymoron is?" he asked.

Paired opposites. But I didn't say it out loud. A burning cold. Jumbo shrimp. Military intelligence.

Nicole Watkins, Lisa's friend, raised her hand. I remember hearing her say that she wrote poetry. "It's when you put together two words that seem opposite in meaning."

"Right you are," Gelbert said.

I was looking at Nicole now and she noticed. She looked back at me and smiled. I turned away and my eyes scanned for the first time the others in the room. A couple of guys were staring at me and turned away. Another girl was looking at me and turned away as well. She looked frightened. I hadn't expected that.

I decided to be the last one out of class when the bell rang. I had survived one period of school. My heart was beating fast now. I felt a panic attack coming on. Maybe I couldn't do this.

Mr. Gelbert was arranging his papers. He said nothing to me. Nicole and Pen Walker were hanging back. When I stood up to leave, they did so as well.

Nicole spoke first. "I know you miss her. We all do."

"Yeah," I said and wanted to say more but couldn't.

"We'll walk you to your next class," Pen said. "What do you have next?"

I checked my schedule and saw that I had Chemistry. "Mrs. Krause. The chemistry lab."

"She's tough," Nicole said. "You good at science?"

"No," I said. "I suck at science."

I felt funny being escorted this way to my class. But it was a good thing. My heart was still racing. My legs felt wobbly as I was delivered to Krause's class. I'd heard bad things about her but as soon as I walked in the room, I understood why she had been on the selected teacher list. She was tough but fair and she wouldn't let anyone in her class get away with anything she didn't like. In her chemistry lab I'd be safe.

Surprisingly, that day, almost all of my battles were internal. Nicole sat with me at lunch. "I want to talk to you about

Lisa sometime. I need to talk to you about her."

"Okay," I said. "But not yet."

"Let me ask you one thing."

"Sure. Just one."

"Did you love her?"

"Yes."

"She was my friend. I'd known her since we were ten. I miss her."

"I miss her too," I said and the tears began to well up in my eyes.

"Sorry," Nicole said. And then she touched my cheek. After that we ate in silence.

I was on my own after that. Walking the crowded hallways. Kids looking at me. Curious. I was both a freak and a celebrity and I wanted to be neither. I tried to avoid eye contact but sometimes I caught a girl staring at me. *Get used to it*, I thought to myself.

The guys were less discreet. Dean and Wentz were a couple of guys that Miranda had introduced me to once. Druggies for sure. They caught up with me on my way to Spanish class. "Must suck to be you," Wentz said right away.

I shrugged. "Yeah, big time."

"What was it like screwing Lisa Conroy?" Dean blurted out.

I realized then that the bastards had found me. I'd been coached by both Louis and my grandmother on this. And between bouts of reading *Heart of Darkness* and *The Sound and the Fury*, I'd been flipping open my *I Ching* book to random passages as Phyllis had suggested. Hexagram 26 had jumped out at me. *Ta Ch'u. The energy that you build up from waiting with awareness will be necessary for the difficulties ahead.*

I said nothing but walked on, my eyes trying to focus on the light coming through the doors at the end of the hallway. It had all been on the news, I realized. People thought they knew everything about me and what had happened. But they knew nothing. Nothing at all.

Chapter 17

I was alone when I walked out of school in the bright sunshine of the afternoon. I didn't see what was out there to greet me. As I shaded my eyes, I think I was having some kind of flashback from much younger days. Back when I'd come out of school and all I could think about was riding my bike or playing soccer with some guys at the park. Back when leaving school in the afternoon filled me with the thrill of freedom. And fun. Right now it all seemed a long way from fun.

I guess they saw me before I saw them. *Action News.* Channel Seven. "He's over here," I heard the woman say. Cindy Something. I saw the *Action News* truck in the background. I saw the satellite dish on top. Capable of live broadcast, I supposed. Once a weather girl, Cindy was now a newswoman. She'd shoved a microphone in my face before outside the courthouse. Her and so many others. Always rude, always insistent. My parents had tried to keep me shielded from the news stories but some got through. Cindy had me pegged for a murderer from day one.

I could have run for one of the buses. Any one would do. I had a feeling the bus drivers wouldn't let on a TV reporter. Instead, I stood my ground. *You'll get past this.* Or the Biblical words of Phyllis: *This too shall pass.*

The sun was still in my eyes so I was squinting. Cindy was right in front of me and her camera guy, lens to the eye socket, was literally running to get in close–I knew how they did it. I knew enough about TV. A wobbly tight shot on anybody's face makes them look nervous and even guilty. I thought of putting my hand up to the lens like the celebrities do when they are sick to death of intrusion. But I knew how that played on TV too. It looked bad.

"Michael Grove," Cindy said, as I stood there, a crowd of students now pulling into a circle for an audience. "Michael Grove, can you tell us how it feels to be back in school after all you've been through?"

The handheld mike was hovering inches before my mouth. I froze. Hawker had trained me, nearly brainwashed me, into not speaking to the media. Any media. "They can do anything with what you say. Anything. They have total control over what they want the audience to believe."

One of my grandmother's favorite expressions, ironic given her current circumstance, was, "When in doubt, just breathe."

I was breathing. Heavily. And the mike was picking up all of it, I'm sure.

Cindy didn't quite know what to do with the dead air. "You must be quite happy to be here today with all your friends."

It was supposed to lead me somewhere. I did a quick scan of the faces around me. I didn't see any friends. I saw a lot of teenagers who had fully believed I had killed the girl I loved. The story had been drilled into them by people like Cindy, professionals whose careers had ascended in coverage of my tragedy. "Friends?" I accidentally asked.

Cindy saw the confusion in my eyes and, realizing she was blowing it, turned to a face in the crowd. A younger guy edging up to the front, wanting to be seen on TV. Cindy asked him, "How do you feel about having

Michael Grove back in your school?"

The kid was a couple of years younger and had a baseball cap on with the phrase *Mo' Money*. He looked straight into the camera as if he'd been waiting for this opportunity but then suddenly seemed to get nervous when he realized he was on TV. The mike was in his face and all he could finally do was shake his head and say, "I don't know, man."

The cameraman was tilting his head back towards me, afraid I would edge away. Figuring I might just run. I thought about running just then. I put it back on a small list of things I wanted to do. Run like the wind. I wanted to feel the wind in my face. But not now. Cindy lowered the mike, dropped her persona, came closer to me and said, like she was my best friend in the world, "Look, I know this is not easy. But now you have a chance to show them you are normal. Can we try again?"

Try again. Um. What did she want me to say? That it was good to be back? Good to have lost more than eighteen months of my life to courtrooms and prison? Good to try to pick up where I left off without Lisa?

I saw Nicole pushing through the crowd, trying to

get to the front, trying to catch my eye. I think she was one of the few in the crowd who knew what I was feeling. Something was starting to emerge and I realized I'd have to talk. Maybe now was the time. What was about to surface was anger. I was torn. Reason said to shut the mouth. Keep it shut. Emotion told me to go volcanic. Give Cindy Whatsherface full frontal feeling. *My life has been ripped away from me, you asshole, and you helped do it. You, the judge, the jury, the viewers, and a lot of these silly turds at this school that you think are my friends.*

The mike was nearly touching my trembling lips, the cameraman had his focus just about as tight as he could on what must have been a contorted, tortured face. I could feel myself shaking, vibrating with anger. But before I could spew the words, I felt a hand on my shoulder. I almost jumped.

"We're pleased to have Michael back with us in school," Mr. Tyson said, looking straight at the camera. "He's decided to pick up where he left off. And now I'm afraid that I'm going to have to ask you to leave."

He said it in a tone of voice he had once used when giving me a lecture about smoking marijuana before classes. He used the same tone of principalian authority on Cindy and her camera guy.

"All we'd like is to give Michael a chance to speak for himself," Cindy's camera guy said.

Tyson was cool as ice. He'd removed his hand from my shoulder. He knew kids didn't like that sort of thing. But it had worked. He had taken charge. I was off the hook.

Cindy looked back at me again, hopeful. She knew she had blown a good chance for a scoop.

"You're on school property," Mr. Tyson said to her again in the coolest of cool voices. "I have to ask you to leave." He too knew that he might appear on TV, that it could be twisted any way the producer wanted to slant it. But he was going the distance.

"It's okay," I said. "I just have one thing to say. Let me say it."

Cindy was back to me, leaning in with her mike. The camera's dead dark eye was on me.

"It's good to be back," I said. "It's good to be back in school."

Cindy waited for more but I refused to give. I had offered up the blandest, most vacuous lie I could have, and then I walked away and got on my old bus. I sat alone in the back and waited as other students boarded the bus. Some stared straight at me, some had the courtesy to pretend they had no interest.

I could see Mr. Tyson ushering the TV people back into their truck. The camera was getting one final parting shot of the bus. And then Pen Walker sat down beside me. "You did good. What a pain in the ass those people are. I haven't watched TV since I was thirteen."

It was an odd thing for a person to say, but maybe not Pen. It reminded me of something Lisa might have said. In fact, I remembered she had said that she never watched TV. "How can you do that?" I asked, assuming that TV was just a part of everyone's everyday life, love it or hate it. How could anyone just *not* watch TV?

"You just turn it off and leave it off," Lisa had said. "Or you simply don't have one in the house."

Pen opened his backpack just then and took out a folded piece of paper. "I was holding off on this, but you might need it."

Even as I was unfolding it, I recognized the handwriting. "What is it?"

"It's a poem, man. It's a poem she wrote that I was going to use in the school's literary magazine. But I didn't."

The words were a blur, but the gentle, feminine handwriting was unmistakable. It was hers.

"It's a poem she wrote for you," he added. "That's what she told me."

I was afraid to read it. Afraid of how it would make me feel, maybe even afraid of what it had to say. "How come she didn't show it to me?"

"I don't know. She said she kept rewriting it. She didn't want you to see it until she got it right."

The bus stopped and Pen got up. "See ya in school tomorrow," he said.

"Yeah, see ya." And he walked down the aisle and was gone.

I folded the poem and put it back in my pocket. And I waited until I was within the safety of my room at home before I dared to unfold it and read the words she had written.

Medicine Walk
(for Michael)

When you believe you are beyond repair
let go.
When you cannot be saved by all your friends
when you cannot be saved by yourself
remember that I love you
and deliver what is left of you
to that place we have shared
in our hearts.

Use whatever means to get close
but then you must walk the final path
and if you cannot walk, then crawl.
It is your only hope.
The word "sacred" could scare you off
so be silent
be there
and do not ask
about why things are
the way they are.

Just promise that we will always share
the sweet geography of us
alive for all time
beyond fear and change,
a quiet place
in the wilderness
of our love.

Chapter 18

The poem stayed with me for days. No. It stayed with me from then onward. It's still with me. When I first read it, I realized I was still in love with Lisa. I still have the poem and I look at her handwriting sometimes. The way she shaped the letters. They are like flowers. Sometimes I just stare at a word. Sometimes I think there is more to the words. *When you believe. When* you believe and *what* you believe rules everything. *You are beyond repair.* That was almost too much.

In my room, with Lisa's poem. Then. I had believed I was already "beyond repair" but I had never found the words. Lisa had written this poem for me. But I didn't know how or why. It was like she knew I would need this message from her–from beyond her death. And it was a poem of instruction. *When you believe you are beyond repair*... you must do these things.

So, as I tried to fall asleep that night, my first night

after my attempt at parachuting back into the world to be normal, I "delivered" what was left of me to that shared place we had found, that sweet geography.

And slept deeply. Then awoke and, for the first time since the day of Lisa's death, I believed repair was possible. I found a small reserve of inner strength that I did not know was there.

Such strength did not fully carry me through a second day of school. But it helped. The second day was not easier. Someone scrawled some words I will not repeat on my locker with a permanent marker. It didn't really make any sense at all but they were words that required janitorial assistance. It was a powerful reminder that there were some in the school who still hated me. If I was not the murderer, I was somehow still an accomplice of a murderer. I was the reason Lisa was murdered.

Be silent. Be there. Lisa's words were the mantra to quell the panic attacks in Chemistry and English.

But it did not help at all when Mr. Tyson showed up in class in the early afternoon and asked me to walk with him out of the classroom.

"It's your grandmother. She's in the hospital. Your

parents called and they said you'd want to be there."

"Is she bad?"

"She's in the hospital. That's all I know. C'mon, I'll drive you."

On the way, Tyson tried in his own way to give me a pep talk. He did it poorly and I liked him even more for that. "You've been dealt a rough hand, Mr. Grove. From what I can see, you are stronger than most. You'll get past this too." Then he handed me rosary beads. I didn't even recognize them at first. "Do you believe in God?" he asked.

"I don't know," I said, taking the rosary beads. "Do you?"

"I don't know. I don't even go to church. But I fall back on it. I grew up Catholic."

"Went to confession?"

"I did."

"What did you have to confess?"

"Impure thoughts. Theft."

"Really?"

"Really. Nothing big."

I looked down at the rosary beads. "What do I do with this?"

"Keep it. Just carry it around. Hold onto it and pray

for your grandmother."

"About the God thing. I think that if I was a real religious type, I'd believe that God was punishing me. Look at what I've been through."

"I thought about that too. I don't know why you or Lisa had to suffer what you did. All I know is that you have a chance to go on. And maybe live a happy life. Do some good."

Tyson was a mystery to me. He really was. Like many kids at school, I had thought he was an arrogant man, an asshole. Instead, he was this other thing. I pocketed the beads and wondered why he believed I could live a happy life. "Happy" and "life" were not two words I could string together in a sentence.

The car came to a stop in front of the hospital. "Room 567," Tyson said. "You want me to go in with you?"

"No. Thanks. I'm okay."

He nodded. "I'll pray for you," he said.

"I thought you didn't believe in God."

"I said I wasn't sure. But it doesn't hurt to pray. Just in case."

"Right. Thanks again."

My parents were in the room. Phyllis was lying on her back with the cup of the oxygen mask over her face. My Dad looked at me and I could tell he'd been crying.

"She's been here for three days," my mother said. "She didn't tell us. Finally the hospital called."

"Her lungs?" I asked.

"And heart."

Phyllis looked like she was sleeping but she raised a hand when she saw me and made a feeble wave.

"Can I talk with her alone?" I asked.

My mom looked at my dad and then he nodded yes and they left the room.

Phyllis pushed a button that raised her head until she was in a sitting position. I noticed the wire attached to her arm and the monitor with a quiet hum beside her. She tried to say something through the mask but the words sounded like mush. Her skin was pale as if something had sucked all the color out of her.

She shook her head back and forth and then lifted the mask off her face and coughed. I sat down in the chair beside the bed.

"You were in school?" she asked.

"Yes. I started going again."

"Good. Do you like it?" Her words were labored.

"What's not to like?" I said sarcastically.

She smiled and laughed a little before having to stop to suppress a fit of coughing. It took some painful seconds for her to recover. "Hexagram 30. *Li. Don't move forward too quickly. Go slow with clarity and composure. Concentration helps.*"

"I remember that one. Do you think I'm moving too fast?"

"No. Just work on staying calm."

I wanted to ask her how she was doing but I knew I wasn't going to get a straight answer. The way she looked was terrible. I almost would not have recognized her had I been walking through the hospital ward.

"Lisa wrote me a poem," I said. "Would you like to hear it?"

"Very much."

So I read her the poem that I was still carrying in my shirt pocket.

"Beyond fear and change," she said. "I like that."

"How sick are you?" I finally asked.

"Sick enough to die if I wanted to."

"Why would you want to?"

"When the breathing is bad, it's very bad. I can't get my breath and I am very, very afraid. It's a terrible feeling. And they say there is a strain on my heart. Lungs and heart–not good. Sometimes it's painful to breathe. So they give me medication. But I'm not sure I want to live like this." She pointed to the oxygen mask lying beside her. "Darth Vader."

"But you can't die," I said. "You can't die because I couldn't handle it. I couldn't stand to lose one more person. Not you."

She lifted the mask to her face and took a couple of breaths from it. "I know," she said. "I've already thought about that. Truth is I'm more afraid of living–like this–than I am of dying. Isn't that peculiar?"

"No," I said. "I've been there. In prison, when I thought I'd be there for years, I thought the same thing. I was reading those books about death. I thought about it and considered the idea of 'release.' Just make the pain go away."

"I remember you wrote me about it. I was worried but you seemed to be dealing with it in a way that was well beyond your years."

"I stared it down. I had lots of time. Lots of time to think."

"I've stared it down too," Phyllis said, looking into my eyes.

"You know why I gave up any thoughts of a quick, easy exit?"

"Yes, I remember. You told me. You wrote that in a letter too. I cried. You said you couldn't do it to your parents. And you couldn't do it to me."

"Right. Exactly. I wanted to do it to punish everyone else. Everyone. I wanted them to see how badly damaged I was. I wanted them to feel bad when they heard about it. But I knew it wouldn't be fair to you and my parents."

"I'm older, you know. I've had a good life."

"That's what I thought you might say."

"But it doesn't get me off the hook, does it?"

"No," I said. "Because I need you. I need to know you are there for me."

"Okay," she said. "I'm not going anywhere until you're ready. I can't live forever but I'll hang in there. The doctors have a couple of more treatments that I've been holding off on."

I reached in my pocket for a handkerchief and discovered the rosary beads. I lifted them out and gave them to my grandmother. She was thoroughly puzzled. "What?" she asked. "I don't get it."

"You're on your way to sainthood," I said. "You might need this."

Chapter 19

Action News ran what they had. Which was not much. I didn't watch it but when we were sitting in the cafeteria the next day, Pen told me that the spin was this: boy wrongly convicted of murder through a miscarriage of justice. Someone should be blamed. "It must make you angry," he said. "How do you deal with it?"

I liked Pen. He was sincere and straightforward. He wasn't the type who I would have chosen for a friend. He and Lisa and Nicole always had some cause going. They were out to save the world. I wasn't that type. In truth, I was the guy always wondering, what's in this for me. I was a for–me person. My tribe made up much of the world's population. But now I was in another tribe. I was in the tribe of victims. If I wanted to, I could live the rest of my life with a big badge. Hell, I didn't even need the badge or the T–shirt or the cap. You could probably read it on my face.

"I don't know if I do deal with it, Pen. Think about it. Who should I blame? The police? The prosecutor? My idiot lawyer? The judge and the jury? The media, for sure. That's a lot of folks to be angry at. I don't know if I have that much energy." I decided not to even mention Miranda.

"I tried putting myself in your shoes. I imagined being you. And I don't think I'd be handling this as well as you do."

"Thanks for the compliment. I'm just not sure I really am handling it."

At school, Pen and Nicole both "looked out" for me. It was a funny feeling, to be watched. Protected even. Mr. Tyson was doing it too. Into the second week, kids had stopped staring at me.

Phyllis had stabilized on the new medication and was allowed to go home. I visited with her and we played Monopoly or threw the *I Ching* sticks or watched documentaries about wildlife on TV. Her favorites involved penguins and birds on remote islands. She still did not look healthy and I knew she wasn't out of the woods. The emphysema and heart problems weren't going to go away.

"I always meant to travel," she said. "But everywhere

I wanted to go was so far away. And too expensive."

"Where did you want to go?"

"Fiji. Micronesia. Bali. Vanuatu. The Andaman Islands."

"Why those places?"

"I don't know. I saw them on world maps. They seemed like impossible places. I guess that was why I wanted to go there. Maybe if I had a million dollars I would have gone."

Phyllis still had me go to the store to buy lottery tickets for her even though she seemed to have lost her naive optimism that one of these times she was going to win.

"Hawker still wants me to sue. A couple of other lawyers have called. I've heard my parents talk about it. I guess we would win. I could buy us a round trip ticket to the Andaman Islands."

"Mine would have to be one way. Besides, I don't think I could handle the travel. Those days are gone."

The phrase echoed within me. *Those days are gone.* "What do you think I should do?"

"About the money?"

"Yes. About making someone pay."

"How would it make you feel, Michael?"

"It would make me feel bad," I said. "I'd hate it."

"Why?"

"I'm not sure. Something to do with Lisa."

"You still miss her?"

"Of course. I think I still love her. How can that be?"

"You haven't fully had a chance to deal with her loss."

"Something like that. But it's more. It's all tangled up with Miranda too. I had really cared for Miranda too. I thought I had been in love with her. But as she changed, I just walked away."

"You believed she was going to drag you down with her."

"I don't know what I believed. I just know that I made some bad decisions. Trying to sue for wrongful conviction wouldn't help anyone. I know that. I received a letter from one of the jurors. She said she was sorry. It was sincere. Isn't that funny? Only one person had the guts to write to me."

"One is better than none," she said. "There's a lot of people in my life I'd like to say I'm sorry to. And I've never done it. Most of us just want to walk away from our mistakes."

"I know," I said. But as I said it, I realized I wasn't

talking about jurors or lawyers. I was thinking about me. Why did I still feel the guilt? And who was it that I needed to say I'm sorry to?

"For each ecstatic instant/ We must pay/In keen and quivering ratio/ to the ecstasy," Phyllis said. "Emily Dickinson said that." Then Phyllis pointed to the unopened pack of real cigarettes on the table.

I picked up the smokes. I hadn't had a cigarette since I forced myself into cold turkey everything in prison. Phyllis studied me. "I can't believe I gave you your first cigarette."

"Hey, what's a grandma for?"

Phyllis leaned over and turned on her oxygen tank and pulled the clear mask over her face. She took a deep breath and pointed to the cigarettes. "You light up one of those things while I have this on, and the whole place will light up like the Fourth of July."

I held the sealed pack of cigarettes up to my nose and smelled the sweet smell of tobacco. It reminded me of Miranda and that scared me. Miranda hadn't smoked when I met her. But that changed quickly. Whenever I had kissed her, there had always been the taste of tobacco on her breath. Sometimes when she and I had smoked weed, we'd cover it up by smoking cigarettes. And each time we'd had sex, we both smoked afterwards. At the time, I had believed it was her leading me into all the forbidden territory. She was the "bad" girl I wanted her to be. I had assumed she was way ahead of me.

But it suddenly occurred to me that maybe I was wrong.

Phyllis looked tired. "Need a nap?" I asked.

"Yes. You can stay if you want."

"No, I need to get some fresh air. Let me help you to bed."

I walked her to her bedroom and felt how frail her body was. I made sure she took her medication and I adjusted the oxygen bottle by the bed. I kept wondering which visit with my grandmother would be my last.

Outside, I checked my watch and discovered it was five-thirty. I didn't want to go home. There was a fire in my head, a madness that would not go away. How did it go? *For each ecstatic instant we must pay.* Crime and punishment. Maybe the crime was in the living. My greatest crime was that I had been the one who ultimately got to walk away.

Not Lisa. Not Miranda.

My parents had insisted I carry the family cell phone. It was in my pocket. Louis had given me his home phone number. He said I could call him any time at work or at home. I pulled his number out of my pocket and dialed.

"Louis?"

"Yep."

"It's Michael."

"You all right?"

"I don't know. I'm mixed up. I can't seem to put the pieces together."

"You want to come over?"

"Maybe."

"Sure."

He explained where he lived and I caught the bus to his neighborhood. Louis had a small neat house with a well–trimmed lawn. His car was in the driveway.

"Come on in," he said.

I walked in and looked around an amazingly immaculate house. It was quite a contrast to the image I had of Louis when he was at work–old coveralls with grease on them and on his bare arms and face.

"You live alone?"

"Now I do. My wife left with the kids when I was in prison. They say that's common. Want something to eat? I hate eating alone."

"Sure," I said. "Let me call my folks and tell them not to wait on dinner."

"Now that's being considerate," Louis said and faded to the kitchen while I called.

After I hung up, I followed him into the kitchen and was shocked to see a table with dishes of steaming vegetables and rice. "Hope you like Indian food," he said.

"Sure."

"Sit. Eat."

"You expecting company?"

"Nope. I do this for myself. Makes for lots of leftovers. Makes me feel like I got a life. But I don't really. Perrier?"

"Huh?"

"Water?"

"Sure."

"So," he said. "How's your grandmother?"

"Not great, but hanging in there."

"Good. Now eat. We'll talk later."

Later was after we had scoffed down curried chicken and rice and lentils and other things that Louis had to provide names for. "My goal is to be a vegetarian. When I worked in the kitchen in Severton, there was another inmate, Luigi, who taught me a thing or two about nutrition and cooking. He had a thing for coriander and tofu. I've been meaning to pick up where I left off then but… well, life gets in the way. And work. So now tell me about why you are here."

"I'm not sure. I just had this feeling that you would be one of the few people who understand what I'm going through. It's weird. I mean, I'm starting to get over the panic attacks, but it's like there's something gnawing at me. Something I'm supposed to do but I don't know what it is. I thought maybe you'd felt this way when you got out."

Louis collected dishes from the table, took them to a dishwasher, and proceeded to load it very carefully. "Michael, first off, remember that you were innocent. I was guilty. I deserved my time. You didn't."

"But how did you feel when you got out? After the freedom part wore off."

"I felt like shit. I'd lost my wife and kids, my job. I ended up with this empty house and I wanted to put my old life back together. But couldn't. I drank some and that didn't help. I tried hanging out with my old buddies but they'd all moved on without me. I was Joe Lonesome for a while. I tried to figure a way to make amends to the people I'd hurt the most. Even the guy who I held up at gunpoint. I traced him and went to talk to him. But he didn't want anything to do with me. So I tried talking to my wife and the kids but I scared them, I guess. My own kids didn't really want anything to do with me. So it was still Joe Lonesome. I even wondered if I'd be better off back inside. All it'd take would be one petty crime and I'd at least have some friends. Luigi was in for life. Your old buddy Eduardo would still be there. And I'd have Skullbones to recommend books. It seemed to make more sense."

"But you didn't do it?"

"No. I got a job fixing people's exhaust systems. And I redecorated." He put his arms up. It seemed like the oddest thing to say. "And then I started doing little acts of kindness for people I didn't know. I reached out.

Sometimes I was wrong and people didn't appreciate it. Other times it did the trick. I'm not saying I did much good. It's just that it felt good trying." He paused and looked up at the ceiling. "But if I could, I'd still want to try to make contact with the people I hurt. I'd start with whoever got hurt the worst and then work my way down the list."

"You made a list?"

"A long one. Kept it in my head in Severton. Nothing written down, though. You know who was first on my list."

I shook my head.

"Me. I was. And I was the toughest son of a bitch to get to, I'll tell you that."

Chapter 20

Nicole was the one who first hinted that Lisa's parents wanted to talk to me. Nicole was smart and she was kind and the death of Lisa had hurt her in some deep, powerful way that sometimes caused her to start crying in school. They had been friends from the time they were young. She truly understood my loss and we had a bond. It was an odd relationship. Like Pen, if she saw trouble–and sometimes it was like a psychic thing–she'd steer me away from it. Through the rest of that school year, I maintained my notoriety where I would have preferred to be anonymous.

There had been a couple of attempts by the media to interview me but I learned that the best thing to do was simply turn and either walk quietly away, or run. Yes, sometimes I actually ran. On one occasion, I had just left the house and was headed to the bus stop to go visit Phyllis. And it was like the TV people had been watching me. They knew where and when I'd leave home. But they stayed far enough away so that I'd be out of range of my parents or an easy retreat back inside.

It was a young reporter from the all–news channel. A kind of media ambush. He had a mike and a cameraman stepped out from behind a tree. I did like those others you've seen on TV. I put my hands up in front of me, shielding my face from the camera. And then I ran.

It felt good to run. It was the beginning of something that was useful to me. I ran half the way to Phyllis's house, surprised that my lungs could work this well and listening to my own breath and heartbeat. I had to ease up and walk the last ten blocks, but by the time I entered my grandmother's living room, I felt better than I'd felt in quite a while.

I didn't know until that evening why the media had wanted to bring me back into the spotlight. But then I heard on the news that there had been another murder in a nearby town. A girl had killed another girl and there had been drugs involved. And this would have prompted an all–news channel to resurrect Lisa's story and rekindle all our pain. That's the way the media worked. For the thousandth time I re–imagined the scene–Lisa there in the tent where we had made love, with a knife wound, and the blood spilling out of her as she died.

My parents bought me running shoes. And sometimes I ran with Nicole who had been on the track team and competed in marathons. She and I were awkward at conversation at the best of times, but having this thing to do–this running–made us closer. Some of her expressions and mannerisms reminded me of Lisa and that was always a bit tough. We spoke haltingly when we ran. Sometimes not at all. And sometimes I noticed our ragged breathing, after we'd gone a fair distance, was perfectly in synch. Sometimes, if she was a bit ahead of me, I'd focus on her pony–tailed hair flipping from side to side. Or sometimes I'd look at her body and think she was sexy. But then I'd look up and away. I didn't want to go there. So I ran faster.

Running made me leaner. And smarter. I was holding my own at school. Keeping out of trouble, doing homework. No weed, no drinking. I almost never watched TV. I didn't play video games. I read voraciously. Nicole and Pen had loaned me a dozen books. Some for new ideas, some for pure escape. I read novels but never murder mysteries.

Nicole invited me over to her house one night and her parents didn't seem too happy to see me but they were polite enough and left us alone in the living room after they went to bed. She wanted me to watch a movie called *Waking Ned Devine.* It was funny and Irish and quirky and I liked it. And then she kissed me. And I was shocked. I hadn't seen that coming. At first I did nothing. But then I kissed her back.

And as I did, I began to cry. "Must have been something in the movie," I said. But I knew it wasn't that. Nicole had broken down a barrier inside me. I was almost afraid of what might happen next. Nicole touched the tears on my face with her fingertips and then put them to her lips, but said nothing. After the movie, we sat there in silent shared awkwardness. "Let's run tomorrow," I said. "Let's see how far we can go."

Hexagram 61, *Chung Fu,* suggests that sometimes you need to *avoid becoming dependent on others. Maintain inner strength and avoid uncertainty.* Phyllis said this was impossible in the world we lived in and that uncertainty was at every step in life. I had begun to think about Nicole when I wasn't with her. But it was different from the way I felt about Lisa. Or Miranda. If Miranda had been lust, and Lisa had been love, then what was this? Friendship? But in each case, it was a kind of dependency and it seemed unavoidable. In my incautious moments, I traced the awful path of circumstances and events that led to Lisa's death and, each time, I became more certain that I had been responsible for the chain of events. They *had* convicted the true killer in the courtroom. I found it harder and harder to take Louis's advice and forgive myself.

And now I was drawing Nicole, a smart, good girl who hoped to someday become a social worker, into my life. I could do her a big favor and drop out of her existence. But I couldn't bring myself to do that. I was dependent on her.

It was a rainy Thursday night when she phoned. "Lisa's parents found her journals," she said. "They said they had hardly touched her room, that everything was still there. But they finally had to deal with it. They read about you."

I swallowed hard but said nothing. I knew Lisa was a writer, I knew she kept a journal, but I didn't know what she put in it. And I expect that she intended to keep them for herself. Not for her parents to read.

"They want to meet with you," Nicole said. "They called me to ask to help set it up."

"I don't think I can," I said. "They were there at the trial. I saw the looks in their faces. They hated me more than anyone in the room. I carried those looks with me into prison. I don't think I could ever face them."

"I know."

"What do you think Lisa wrote about in her journals?" I asked.

"Everything. She said that in writing anything, you must be perfectly honest. She never showed them to me. But I knew Lisa."

"What good would it do to meet her parents?"

"I'm not sure."

"Do you think she wrote about everything we did?"

"Probably."

"I can't meet with them. Tell them I'm sorry."

Nicole seemed disappointed in me suddenly. "You loved Lisa, didn't you?" she asked. There was hurt in her voice.

I said nothing.

"And Miranda, what about her? I can't see what you saw in her. What was that all about anyway?" There was anger now in her voice. This was unlike Nicole. She had always been so accepting of everything. What had triggered this?

I knew I couldn't tell her the truth. I couldn't tell her that, once upon a time, I had loved Miranda too. "I don't know," I said. "I'm sorry." But Nicole had already hung up.

The next day Nicole acted as if the conversation had never happened and she never mentioned Lisa's journals or her parents again. But Lisa's parents called my house once and left a message on our machine to call them. I erased the message before my parents heard it and did not return their phone call. When they called a second time, their number was blocked and, curious as to who it was, I answered.

"Michael, this is Lisa's father," I heard the man say. "We'd like to talk to you. It's important. Can we come to your house?"

"No," I said.

"Please. It's important. We need to do this for Lisa."

"I don't know what you mean."

"Please meet with us and I'll explain."

My hand was trembling. Right then I was thinking about what Louis had told me about forgiveness. And I was thinking that this might somehow clear the air with Nicole. But most of all I now knew that meeting her parents would help me reconnect with Lisa. And I desperately wanted Lisa–anything to do with Lisa–back into my life.

"Okay," I said. "I'll come to your house. I'll head over there now."

"Thank you," he said.

Chapter 21

I ran the twenty or so blocks to Lisa's house. I could not have walked there. And I did not want my parents involved. I knew that if I could just get my legs moving and my lungs working hard, I could avoid thinking about it, avoid any second thoughts, and just do this thing.

I arrived sweaty and panting. Lisa's father, who looked like he'd aged twenty years since I'd seen him last, answered the door. He said nothing about the shape I was in. "Thanks for doing this. Come in."

I tried to slow my breathing down but my heart continued to beat wildly.

"Sit down," Lisa's father said as his wife came into the living room. She tried to give me eye contact but quickly looked away. On the coffee table was an open photo album with pictures of Lisa as a little girl.

"We do this sometimes," her father said with an air of defeat and sadness. "We look at the pictures of our little girl. It still doesn't seem real that she's gone." He closed the album and set it under the table. From underneath he picked up a pair of bound writing booklets and set them on top.

"The journals?" I asked.

"Yes," Lisa's mother replied. "They were very personal. We would have never violated her privacy if…"

"I understand," I said. "Lisa loved to write. She told me about her journals. But she never showed me anything."

"They weren't intended for anyone to read, of course. We didn't even know they were in her room until recently."

"It must have been very difficult to do this."

"Torture," her mother said. "But it was necessary."

"You're in there, Michael," her father said. "In the last year of her life, there is a lot about you."

"She loved you," her mother said. "We know that now."

I guess I wasn't expecting that. They should have known all along that Lisa loved me and I loved her. They should have known I could not have killed her. But I had showed them another version of me back then. They believed I was trouble. The neighbors had talked. I had liked it back then that people thought I was trouble. The clothes I wore, the look about me. I knew the messages I gave adults and I liked the way it made me feel.

"Did you feel the same way?" her father asked.

"I loved her, if that's what you mean."

"Then, when she died, you felt the same way we did."

"I think so."

"Then I'm sorry for you. Everything must have been terrible for you."

"Can I?" I asked, touching the journal.

Lisa's mother nodded. I flipped open the journal and could not focus on the words, only the handwriting, that same elegant handwriting I had seen in the poem. My eyes focused and I realized I had opened to a page of Lisa writing about us. About making love in her room. I turned the page quickly and realized that both of them had read every word in these journals, knew every intimate detail about Lisa and me. At first, I guess, I felt embarrassed, but then a shock wave of emotion slammed into me. The wonder and beauty I had felt with her in my arms. And then the overwhelming sense of loss, the pain, and the grief.

"We want you to take them and read them," her mother said, shocking me. "But we'd like them back."

"Why?"

"Because we think they might help with what you are going through," she said.

"But you've read these, right? You've read everything. How come you don't hate me?"

"Because Lisa loved you," her father said. "And we think you loved her. And it's not just us who lost her. We know that now."

"We were so wrong," Lisa's mother said.

I looked down at the journals and didn't know what to say.

Lisa father cleared his throat. "I wasn't going to say this but I need to get it out."

"Don't," his wife said. "You promised you wouldn't."

"Sorry," he said. "It's been burning inside me. I need to tell him." Then he paused and tried to muster some inner strength. "Back then," he continued, "back before the trial, I was thinking that I didn't trust the legal system. And I thought the best thing would be to kill you myself. I thought about it a lot. Went so far as applying for a license to buy a gun. I never bought one. But I believe I was capable of doing it."

His words didn't shock me, really. I knew what I represented to so many people in the town and I understood what he was saying. He was waiting for some response from me. He was thinking I'd be appalled. I wasn't.

"I think in some ways it would have been easier. On me, that is."

"But he didn't do it," his wife said in his defense. "He didn't even come close. I kept saying to him, 'Then what about me? What happens to me after that?'"

"I couldn't do that to my wife," he said.

I sat silently, holding Lisa's journals to my chest, wondering if I'd have the ability to read them and what it might do to me. "Can I see some of your photos of Lisa?"

"Sure, you can," her mother said, and pulled up the photo album and opened to pictures of Lisa's last year on earth.

Lisa was very much alive in each photo. Her spirit and grace came across in every image and it seemed inconceivable that her life had been taken away from us all. I turned the pages very slowly and felt my heart at last beginning to slow its fevered pace. I felt something come over me that was profoundly sad but beautiful. And when I came to the last page of photos–not the end of the album, but the last page of photos I turned the empty pages that came after. The unfilled pages, the ones that would have held pictures of Lisa and her life, had she lived.

And then I closed the album and touched its cover.

I opened one of the journals now and stared at a page. *I can tell that in Michael's heart there is love. I can tell by the way he kisses me that he is kind and loving.* I turned the page and there was more but I did not continue to read.

I stood up and placed the journals back on the table. "Thank you for sharing this," I said. I didn't know what else to say. And I left.

Chapter 22

Mr. Tyson gave the go–ahead for me to attend the graduation ceremony and receive a diploma, but I didn't really graduate. There would be summer school classes to take. The ceremony had a kind of slo–mo, underwater feeling to it all. I was there but not there. I wondered if this was the way my life was going to play out. There but not there. Graduating but not really graduating. Living but not really alive.

They let Nicole give a little speech about Lisa and I had prepared myself for that. I faded deep into myself. I know my parents fought hard to hold back tears. Lisa's folks were not in the audience. And Miranda. Nobody was saying a word about her. There would be no graduation ceremony for Miranda.

My name was called and my feet felt heavy as I clumped up to the stage and shook hands with Mr. Tyson. You watch the others go up before you and you know your turn is coming but when you actually hear your name, it all feels so strange. Who is this person walking up to receive his high school diploma? Wasn't I just a little kid on a tricycle not so long ago? Wasn't I still pissing in my pants and blubbering when I fell and scraped a knee?

I almost thought Mr. Tyson was going to give me a hug. I didn't want that so maybe he caught my signal. Or maybe he knew it was better not to draw too much attention to me. The document was handed over, the applause faded, and I was off the stage. Wondering what I was going to do with the rest of my life.

Phyllis was there with my parents, her oxygen tank in tow. It was a sad scene. She was fading. When I visited her, she kept prepping me for what was ahead. "I'm on borrowed time, as they say," she kept reminding me. And she meant it.

Louis was in the audience as well. I had invited him. He had been teaching me to cook. I knew a bit about herbs and spices. And I could make pasta from scratch. After the ceremony, he found me and shook my hand enthusiastically. He saw the deer–in–the–headlights look on my face and tried to coach me back into normality. "You're going to do just fine, son. Keep a level head and keep your feet on the ground. Now I gotta get back to work." And he left.

Nicole found me in the parking lot and took my hand, then wrapped her arms around me and hugged me to her.

Nicole.

I need to tell you about Nicole.

It was nothing like Miranda. And it was not like Lisa. We were friends. Sad friends who had shared a loss. Nicole had helped me adjust to school and ran interference–sometimes when I didn't even realize it–steering me away from trouble that was looking for me. We studied together and sometimes we kissed. Sometimes we'd go for long walks or we'd run together. I had to force myself to run but I always felt a little better while I was doing it. We'd run to the river and sometimes just sit there on the grass. We'd make out but I never let it get beyond the basics. Everything about sex and sexual attraction scared me. I explained that to Nicole and she understood.

The night of graduation, Nicole and I didn't go to any

of the parties. I wasn't really invited to any but she was. I suppose we could have shown up together but I didn't want to go. Nicole's parents surprised me by saying that I could stay the night–the two of us would stay in the living room. Maybe they thought this was the safest of all the options. They didn't mean that I was to *sleep with* their daughter. But they were okay if I *slept there* that night.

We split a bottle of wine and her parents didn't even seem to mind that. We watched a couple of Jack Nicholson DVDs–*As Good as it Gets* and *Something's Gotta Give*. And after everything got quiet in the house, I kissed her and held her to me. "I feel like I need you in my life," I said, "but I don't want to hold you back."

"I haven't decided which university I'm going to yet. I may not be going away after all."

"I think you should."

"You want me to?"

"It's not like that. I want you here. But I can't make you do that."

My summer was summer school. My teachers, I am sure, had been given instructions to make sure I made up the work I'd missed so my graduation would be legitimized. They all knew it would be best if I were not around the school for any part of another school year. Lisa's death and the whole sorry story that surrounded it would not be forgotten, but it would be a thing of the past.

I almost gave up on summer school when my grandmother died. I almost gave up on everything.

Phyllis was having a harder and harder time breathing. She was back in the hospital and taking heavy medication to help her heart and to keep her blood thin. My dad went to stay with her for hours every single night. My mom would go see her at least once during the day. I preferred to visit her on my own and sometimes she was too tired to talk. She would look at me, though, and hold my hand. I'd randomly turn to a page in her *I Ching* book and read.

"Hexagram 38 *K'uei: Whatever is lost will return when the time is right. Remaining open to that possibility is the key.* Hexagram 49 *Ko: Hold steadfast to the middle way. Don't attempt too much change too soon.*"

And then she got better. Or so it seemed. Phyllis returned home and I went there every day after school. One day she seemed almost as energetic as before. She could take off the mask for a twenty–minute conversation.

"I wish my father were here," she said out of the blue. She pointed to the shelves of books that ran floor to ceiling. "He was a professor of literature. He gave me the love of books–much like yours–the desire to read anything, far and wide. He slept in chairs, a book in his lap. I didn't know that was an odd thing. I thought all fathers did it. I don't think he slept with my mother very often. In the morning, I'd find him asleep in his reading chair and I'd wake him up. And he would thank me."

Then Phyllis talked about her husband who had died, a subject she had been strangely silent on over the years.

"Your grandfather loved me but he never understood me. I don't think I married him out of love. I married him out of need. I wanted to move away from home. I wanted the life I saw others had. He was kind and dependable. I broke his heart many times. He didn't understand why I did the things I did. Neither did I."

She showed me a photo of him. In it, he was young–twenty–something–and he looked nervous and uncertain. Possibly even scared. "I look a little like him, don't I?" I asked.

"Yes." She nodded.

"How did you two meet?"

"It was a blind date."

"Really?"

"Yes. Friends set us up. I didn't expect it to work."

"But you were open to the possibilities."

She looked at his photo and then back at me. "I wasn't sure I really loved him until he died. And then I realized how deeply I felt. Isn't that a great pity?"

I handed her back the photo and she placed it on the table beside her.

"Life is all about change. We cling to what we know and what we have, and then we lose it, and then we regret not having it and try to replace it by finding and clinging to something else."

"Which hexagram is that?"

"Hexagram Phyllis. The hard part is learning how to lose what you love gracefully and move on. To avoid letting the loss stop you in your tracks."

"I haven't really been able to let go of Lisa. Why is that?"

"Because of the way you lost her. Because you cared deeply."

"Why did I not want to read her journals?"

"I think because you knew that it would bring her memory more alive in you. It would put her back in the middle of your life and some part of you knows you have to move on. Remember that poem of hers you read?"

"Sure."

"That was her saying goodbye to you. But you never had the opportunity to say goodbye to her."

"Did you get to say goodbye to my grandfather?"

"Yes. He was sick for a while and then I realized he wanted me to give him permission to let go."

"And you did that?"

"I did it for him. I told him I would be okay. I told him he could go. Sometimes people hang on for others."

I saw the tiredness in her now. I understood what she was saying and knew that it took quite a bit of her strength to say this to me. I was supposed to say something. I was supposed to give her permission to die. But I couldn't do it.

"But you're getting better, right? Today you seem much healthier. Is it the new medication?"

She shrugged and pulled me to her. "The doctors seem to think I'm one for the record books. Should have been dead long ago. But look at me. Still kicking."

Phyllis died that night in her sleep. She had held on as long as she could, I suppose. I regretted not giving her the comfort she wanted, the permission. And I hoped she would forgive me, wherever she went to. I viewed her casket but did not go the funeral. Instead, I stayed home and read from a pile of books she had given me.

And in the morning, I went back to my classes at summer school. That was the best I could do to let her know that I was going to be okay without her, that I'd find others to help me sort out the painful threads of my life. And that I understood that life is about change, it is a book of changes, a book detailing what we find, what we cling to, and what we lose. And then, for those who learn how, we move on.

Chapter 23

I remember that the thing I liked most about that summer was mowing the lawn. I don't know why and I know it doesn't sound that thrilling. But I liked it. I liked the noise of the mower engine; I liked the neat, straight lines of mowed grass. I liked the repetitive nature of the job. I didn't even mind the scowls from Sudsy next door. I mowed our lawn more often than anyone in the neighborhood. And in the evenings, if I wasn't visiting with Louis or Nicole, I read from the collection of books left by my grandmother.

I read *The Last Temptation of Christ* by Nikos Kazantzakis. I read John Irving, George Orwell, and Anton Chekhov. There was one of Chekhov's short stories called "Gooseberries," which concerned a kind of longing for something you can never have. I didn't understand the story the first time or the second, but I read it again and I got it. It was the way I felt. I longed for something that

I could never have. And I believed I would be like this for the rest of my life. I read F. Scott Fitzgerald. I cried in the middle and at the end of *Tender is the Night*. I was blown away by the poetry of Dylan Thomas. I didn't like Ernest Hemingway but I read him anyway.

And I found myself in awe at how often writers wrote about loneliness and despair. But reading also made me feel connected to my grandmother and to her father, who had once owned many of these books, a man I had never met. And it made me feel close again to Lisa, too.

I completed summer school in July. I had been a good student. The teachers had made it easy for me. My graduation was fully legitimate. I could now "get on with my life," as Mr. Tyson put it. On my last day of school, he hugged me–right in front of the other teachers. Some of them appeared shocked. Then he asked me to step into his office.

I sat in a seat where I had once been before, long ago in another life, when I had been called before the principal because I had gone to class after toking up outside. I had been high even as I sat there. Tyson was stern and direct. Now he was different.

"You did well. Some people around here thought you couldn't do it," he said.

"This part was easy. It's the rest I'm not so sure about."

"It might get easier."

"Here's hoping."

Then ensued an awkward silence. Tyson was waiting for me to say something else. So I did. "Why did you go out of your way to help?"

"Because I thought it was my job."

I shook my head. "The other teachers, they were mostly just doing their job. You were watching out for me. Why?"

"I'm not sure whether to tell you the truth. Someone gave me a break once when I'd made a big mistake. And it made all the difference. I thought that if you could finish school, if I could convince you to hang in there, you'd make it after that on your own."

"You still think that?"

"Yes. I think you'll find your way."

"Then how come it doesn't feel like that?"

"Because you're still hurting. Still confused."

"When does that go away?"

"Maybe never. I lost my son when he was four years old. This was over ten years ago but I think about him every day. And it's still painful."

Something lined up in my head just then. Fitzgerald, Thomas Wolfe, Kazantzakis, something Phyllis had read to me from her *I Ching* book and more. Some coming together of ideas, emotions that had to do with that longing, that loneliness, that hurt that never really goes away. Let's call it human suffering. But it was attached to something else. The need to connect, sometimes even the need to reach out and help someone else in need. A chill went down my spine and I could not speak.

Mr. Tyson cleared his throat. "So... um... what are you going to do next?"

"I never think of the future," I quoted. "It comes soon enough."

"I think I've heard that before."

"Albert Einstein," I said.

"Good one. A writer named Edmund Burke said, 'You can never plan the future by the past.' And I think that is true in your case."

"My past does not go away. I live it every day." I said

this without realizing how similar it was to what Tyson had revealed about himself.

"I know," he said. "But we learn to go on."

With that he stood up and so did I. He shook my hand and looked directly into my eyes like we were old friends, like we'd been through some important ordeal together. "My door's always open," he said.

I doubted I'd ever, ever set foot back in the school but I appreciated it. "Thanks," I said.

As I walked back out into the warm, humid summer afternoon, I recognized something had changed. I couldn't name it or even say if it was good or bad. It was just different and I didn't know why. The color of the sky, the way the leaves were on the trees. The sound of car tires on asphalt. The memory of my grandmother, who I would never see again.

And then I stopped dead in my tracks. I realized one thing for certain. *I had no idea what would happen next.* I had no real plans as to what I would do with the rest of my life. But I had made up my mind about one thing. I dialed Nicole's number on my cell phone and asked her to meet me by the swings in Veterans' Park. I breathed a sigh of relief when she answered and agreed to meet me.

The park was strangely devoid of mothers and children and no kids were on the swings, so we sat on them but did not swing back and forth.

"Are you all right?" she asked. I guess I was acting a bit weird. Even for me.

"Yeah, I'm just feeling a little shaky."

"It was even implied when she said something like, Anything I can do to help?"

Nicole was kind and forgiving. About everything. We kissed sometimes and sometimes I felt passionate about her. Sometimes I felt like I wanted to make love with her. She'd said it was okay if we did. It was even implied when she said something like, *Anything I can do to help?* Sometimes I even thought that's all I needed to feel better, to get on with my life. Maybe all I needed was to get laid and everything would be all right. The old me, still thinking that.

But we had not made love. I had always been the one to call the limits.

"Nicole, I really care for you," I began. A poor start, I suppose. She read me like a book.

"I know what you're going to say. I've been expecting this but I'm not sure I'm ready for it."

"Nicole, I do care for you. And I lean on you. I use you to help me get through the day. I think you are wonderful. But don't stay here and go to the community college. Go to university like you had planned."

"But it's so far away."

"I know. But don't stay here for me. Don't let me hold you back."

"It's funny the way you say it because sometimes I think I'm the one leaning on you. You are my connection to Lisa and that connects me to so much about my childhood. And leaving you behind would be like losing all that. And you too."

"We have a powerful bond, I know that. Part of me wants to always have you there. To go to. To talk to. To keep me from going insane."

"The whole world is insane. You and I have something that makes sense."

"I know what you mean. But now it's time for you to move on. And it's time for me to–I don't know–figure out something."

Nicole pushed off from the ground and began to swing back and forth. She looked like a little girl, the way she did it. I didn't know what to do but just sit there and wait for her to slow down and stop. When she did she had a look on her face that I cannot describe. "Michael, make love to me. My parents aren't home. We can go there."

"Are you sure this is the right thing?"

"I think it's the right thing for me."

"Why?"

"I don't know. I'll try to explain to you. After."

It was her first time. For me, it was the first time since Lisa. And it wasn't easy. I couldn't do it at first. I tried but there were problems. But Nicole was insistent and patient and sexy. She was determined to make this happen. And as we became more passionate and I found myself losing control–losing myself in the act–I felt like it was the right thing. I realized it was the right thing for both of us.

Afterwards, we lay there on her bed, naked and sweating. She traced a line in the wetness across my chest and I kissed her. At that moment I felt at peace. I knew it would not last and I wondered about myself. Was this it? All I needed was sex and I'd feel human again? Could it be that simple?

But I knew it wasn't that simple. I felt like I wanted to tell Nicole that I did love her, that I didn't want her to go away to university. I wanted this afternoon to last forever. We were outside of time and without guilt and without shame, and it felt wonderful.

"The loneliness is gone," I said.

"I'm glad. And I'm glad we did this."

"All those books I've been reading. So much loneliness and longing. And it all seems like it's so easy to make it go away."

"Yes. You can make it go away for a short time. And that's what we did."

"I think I do love you," I said. These were not the right words, but these were the ones I could say.

"And I think I love you. But you're right: we both need to move on."

When she said it, I started to cry. It shocked me and I suddenly felt so vulnerable and strange, lying there naked on the bed. But I also felt a monumental release of something in my chest. I turned over and pushed my face into the pillow as I tried to sort out what I was feeling. She ran her hand down my back.

When I sat back up to look at her, I saw one small tear running down her face. "You're beautiful," she said.

"So are you."

Chapter 24

I wonder sometimes what would have happened if I had never seen the letters–the ones from Miranda that had arrived over the summer. The ones my parents kept hidden from me. I wonder if my life would have been easier or more difficult, simpler or more complicated. Three had arrived and my parents had decided to shield me from whatever they contained. They did not open them but they did not throw them away. Instead, they were locked away in a security box my father had in their bedroom closet.

The fourth letter found its way to me because I happened to get the mail that day. I arrived home and my parents had decided to go out to dinner, just the two of them. I was on my own for a while. There was no return address on the envelope but I thought I recognized the handwriting and I noticed the postal cancellation: Woodvale. I opened it on the spot.

Dear Michael,

It does not surprise me that you didn't answer my other three letters. And I'm not sure why I am writing to you again but you know what it feels like to be locked away and isolated from everything you once knew. There is so much I want to say to you but I'm afraid I'll never have that chance. I've tried to explain in those other letters but I don't blame you if you threw them away without reading them. Everyone tells me I should not try to communicate with you, that this is a bad idea. But here I am again, reaching out to you. I think you might be the only one who can save me. I just don't know what else to do.

Miranda

Miranda. Miranda. The images that flooded my brain were of the times she and I had spent together. The getting–to–know–each–other times. The good times. Taking chances. Pushing each other's limits as we explored the great list of forbidden things we were both so attracted to. When you are sixteen, you expect to live forever, you expect that nothing bad will happen to you, no matter how far you push it. You think the adult world is a dull conspiracy of lies, propaganda, rules, and limitations all created to ruin your good times and your oh–so–important explorations of the body, the mind, and the soul.

Miranda and I had been smug in our self–righteous explorations. Both of us were smart and we'd used our intelligence to justify all the things we did. And then I started to see that we needed to be careful, that there were *limits* we needed to impose on ourselves. After that, things changed.

My neighbor, Sudsy, pulled into his driveway just then and saw me sitting down on the front steps, my head in my hands. I caught the look on his face briefly before he turned away. From the first day home, Sudsy's look stayed with me. It said it all. What some people would think about me forever. It burned into my psyche and would not go away. And there he was again, the accuser, pulling into his driveway at this critical moment. He got out of his car and went into his house.

My parents' dinner had gone badly. Something my father had eaten at the Italian restaurant had not settled well. It would be a tough evening for them both.

I was sitting at the kitchen table when they came in. I hadn't eaten. I had been alone with my thoughts and they were a jumble of memories. Miranda's letter sat on the table before me. My parents understood immediately.

"She shouldn't be writing to you," my mother blurted out.

"Can I see the other letters?"

"What other letters?" my father said, holding his stomach and looking more than a little sick.

"I think there are three," I said. "From Miranda."

"We threw them away," my mother responded.

"They were to me. You had no right to do that." I understood precisely what they had done. And why. But I still harbored a bitter-tasting anger that rose within me and often I had no one to direct my anger at. Parents are good targets. Close and easy to aim for. Right then, I think I hated them for having robbed me of something important. They studied my face. I folded and unfolded the letter in my hand.

"We didn't throw them away," my father said at last. "We hid them. I don't think you should read them."

I contained my anger. I took a deep breath. "Could I

have them please?"

My parents looked at each other and then my father said, "I'll get them."

When he returned, he set them before me. They were unopened.

"You didn't read them?"

"No," my mother said. "It didn't seem right."

I picked them up and looked at them. I looked at the handwriting. And the line from the letter I had already opened echoed in my fevered brain. *I think you might be the only one who can save me.*

I said nothing more but went to my room and read in sequence the three letters that had arrived over the summer. The first had come just about the time of my high school graduation. It was almost incoherent and I had to read it over a few times before I realized how troubled Miranda was. She was trying to explain something about crystal meth. She was trying to get me to understand what had happened to her after we broke up. But it was like an entirely different take on what I had believed to be true. She had liked what the meth did for her. So did I. But I saw the dangers. And I backed off. She didn't.

I thought we had both just moved on. But it wasn't like that for her.

The second letter was more analytical and riddled with anxiety and guilt. Her mood was dark, her time in Woodvale was making her crazy.

In the third letter she mentioned for the first time that she was thinking about suicide. It was postmarked August 20. And now it was September.

September is, for many, a month of dramatic change. Nicole had gone away to university as originally planned. She e–mailed me almost every day. She said she missed me but that the campus was very exciting. She had already joined a group called Students for Social Justice. And that made me think of Lisa. Lisa would have loved university and a chance to meet up with other social activists. I knew that Nicole had done the right thing for her by going away to a bigger school. And she had done the right thing for me too. We had set each other free.

In late August, I took my first job, working with Louis at the muffler shop. I did not want to go to university or community college. Maybe later but not now. I wanted a job I could do that involved something physical. I wanted to get dirty at work. Louis pulled some strings. I was now his assistant. He was probably the only person in my life who understood me. At least that's what I believed.

Louis and I talked while we tore off old rusty tailpipes and I located new parts from the warehouse. The other men on the job treated me fairly–which is to say they pretty much left me alone, or sometimes talked to me about their families or girlfriends or how someday they hoped to win the lottery. Nobody ever mentioned anything about the murder or about my conviction.

I liked having someplace to go to in the morning. I liked the feel of the clean overalls I put on each day. And I liked fixing things, although I had never been very mechanical. Each car had a problem. Our job was to fix it. Make it right. You drove your noisy, exhaust–leaking vehicle into our bay and we ripped off what was corroded and faulty and we fitted the car with muffler and pipes that were new. And you drove away a car that was safer and quieter. Two weeks into the job and Louis had taught me to use an air gun and an acetylene torch.

And one September morning I told Louis about the letters.

"She's crying out for help, Michael. But I'm not sure you should get involved. You're the last person who wants to get tangled up with that."

"But I missed something back there. I didn't know what was happening to Miranda. I dropped out of her life just when she needed me most."

"You dropped out so she didn't drag you down. What was it she was taking?"

"Crystal meth."

Louis shook his head. "Poor man's cocaine, we used to call it. Big rush, big high, big–headed feeling that everything is going great. Then, look out."

"I think she was high in school a lot. You should have seen the creeps she was hanging out with."

"Crystal users are a jittery lot, believe me. The stuff keeps you awake so you don't get much sleep. If you get tired at all, you want to take more to get that edge back. If you ease off, your brain tells you to get back on the freight train and ride. Then paranoia kicks in. Some people get violent. It's still you, but a freakier, nastier you than the old civilized self."

"You've tried it, I take it?"

"Oh, yeah. Brother, I tried it. And liked it. Been there, done that. The thing about meth is that it's very inexpensive and readily available. I didn't think suburban kids were into it that much. Thought you had your weed and ecstasy and cocaine and all them designer drugs."

"We pretty much had everything. You just had to ask around. Miranda was used to getting whatever she wanted."

"And now she wants you to do what?"

"I don't know. Write to her? Talk to her?"

"She's straight now, at least, I reckon. But do you really want to do this to yourself? You want to go down that path?"

"I'm scared, Louis. I'm really scared."

"Then just walk on. Do nothing and maybe it will all go away. You get another letter, don't open it."

"But I still feel responsible."

"I know. But do you have any idea what this would look like to everybody out there?"

"I'm not sure I care much about what people think of me anymore."

"And what exactly is it you are trying to do?"

"She's reaching out. I haven't done anything yet. But one part of me wants to do this thing. I want to go talk to her."

"You want to what?"

"I want to go there to Woodvale and talk to her."

"My advice is to run in the opposite direction."

"But I can't do that," I said. "I just can't."

Chapter 25

Maybe I had read too many novels. Maybe that made me feel like my life had to go somewhere. There was a story and it had to continue. I wasn't looking for an ending but looking for some way to thread together the lunatic sequence of the events of my life and make it add up to something.

I had a feeling that my plot, my life, was being guided by a trail of paper. The proverbial paper trail. And the words that went along with that paper. Phyllis and her *I Ching*. Skullbones and his books. The books I inherited from Phyllis's father, my great–grandfather who I had never met. Lisa's poem that triggered so much within me. Lisa's journals that I myself did not read. (How similar to my own parents–shielding me from those letters from Miranda but not willing to break the code of privacy of the letters themselves.) And now that I had read Miranda's letters, I had the compulsion that I now had to do something. Hexagram 45 (*Ts'Ui*) says: *You will feel the desire for unity and feel at the same time restricted in your actions. Find help from like–minded people. Tears will end and there will be positive results.*

With my first telephone attempt to speak to someone in authority at Woodvale, I was shunted from office to office until I found myself speaking to Miranda's counselor, a woman named Sharon Elgard. I told her who I was. She said she knew about the letters.

"How is Miranda?" I asked.

"She is serving her time as well as can be expected," was the unrevealing answer.

"Do you think she is at risk?"

"I don't know what you mean," Sharon said, although I knew she did.

"In her letter, she sounded desperate."

"I'm not really at liberty to speak to you about this."

"I know," I said. "I understand. But I really think I need to talk to her."

The line was silent.

"I know this must sound crazy," I said. "You know

who I am, right?"

"Yes, I know."

"I can promise you, I have no desire to harm Miranda. I want to help her."

"Only family have visiting privileges here. We sometimes make exceptions, but you'd have to have permission from both her parents and from the director here. And in your case that's not likely."

"Why?"

More silence, and then finally, "Miranda confessed to murdering your girlfriend. And now you want to talk to Miranda. We'd call that a potentially damaging encounter."

"But what if her parents thought it was a good idea?"

"Good luck on that one."

"But will you speak to me again after I've met with them?"

"Yes," she said in very professional tone. "But I'll need to hear from them first."

I did not speak of any of this to my parents. Louis, however, knew what I was up to. He even knew about Miranda's father, a fairly powerful corporate lawyer. A man used to getting his way. "You're playing with fire," Louis said. "The man will find a legal way to shut you out and keep you out."

"I'll talk to him," I said. "I'll make him understand."

I called Miranda's house and spoke first to her mother. She hung up on me. Then I looked up her father's law office and took the bus there.

"Do you have an appointment?" the secretary asked.

"No. I need to speak to Mr. Morgan about his daughter, about Miranda."

She looked at me closely now and recognized who I was. "He's in a meeting with a client," she said.

"I'll wait."

"Maybe you shouldn't be here," she said warily. I could only guess what might be going through her mind.

"I'd appreciate it if you didn't throw me out."

Now she looked a little nervous and confused. So I sat down in a chair and opened a copy of *Fortune* magazine. I stared at an article called "Guerrilla Capitalism" and turned the pages. I stalled when I came to an unlikely quote by an American president. Dwight Eisenhower was quoted as saying, "A wise man doesn't lie down on the tracks of history to wait for the train of the future to run over him." It almost could have been something from the *I Ching*. I flipped through the pages and found myself looking at advertisements for mutual funds, expensive watches, retirement communities, and computers. It was like a portal into a world I knew nothing about. The secretary left the office briefly but returned and sat back down at her desk without even looking at me.

After thirty minutes, the inner office door opened and a man wearing a dark suit and carrying a leather briefcase walked briskly through the waiting room and left. As soon as he was gone, a uniformed security guard walked in. He stood there and said nothing. The office door opened again and Miranda's father walked into the room. He obviously had been prepared. He had been informed that I was here.

"Can I come into your office? I'd like to talk to you about Miranda."

"We can talk here," he said. He knew that he couldn't just tell me to go away. He probably already knew I had tried to talk to his wife. Mr. Morgan nodded to his secretary and she left the room. The security guard stayed.

I felt intimidated but I was determined to move forward.

"I think your daughter is considering harming herself. I think I can help."

He sat down at his secretary's desk and clenched his hands. I saw the muscles tightening in his jaw. He was a man used to getting his way, of waving his hands or throwing some money at a problem or turning it over to someone else to fix. I saw anger in him but also confusion and pain. He looked at the security guard, "You can go. We'll be okay. Thanks for coming."

The guard nodded. "Sure thing. Hit the speed dial on the phone if you need me. I won't be far." And he left.

"When I first met you, I knew you were bad news," he said. "Miranda knew you were the type of boy who would really piss me off. But I couldn't say anything. She was used to getting her way. About most everything."

"This is not about then. It's about now. She wrote to me. She thinks I can help somehow."

"She hardly talks to her mother and me. She's closed herself down so much. I don't know how much longer she can handle it in there."

"My parents hid her letters at first. I only found out

recently she was trying to get in touch with me."

"But why would she write to you? And why would you want to get involved?"

"I don't know."

"I think they may consider letting her out in maybe five more years. We've been working on this since she turned herself in. It was the drugs."

"I know about the drugs. That was one of the main reasons we split up. She was getting deeper into it and I didn't want to go that far."

Mr. Morgan looked angry again. "Then why the hell didn't you try to help her? Why didn't you tell us or do something?"

"Because she would have thought I was a traitor, that's why."

"And I suppose you were a knight in shining armor?"

"No, I was just a guy who decided to move on."

"And let my daughter destroy herself?"

"Something like that. And that's why I'm here."

"Jesus," he said. "She wasn't even out of high school. Do you think a thing like this ever goes away?"

"No. I don't think so."

"I curse myself for not paying attention."

"Maybe there was nothing you could do."

"No, I could have paid attention. I could have noticed that she was changing before my eyes, that she was destroying herself."

"My grandmother died this summer," I said, not exactly knowing why I said it. "We talked a lot before she died. She smoked quite a bit and she knew it would kill her and it did. But it didn't stop her from wanting to smoke right up to the end. She was big on giving advice and a lot of it was wrong. But sometimes she hit the nail on the head. Here's what she told me. She said, 'Sometimes the single most difficult thing for you to do is the thing you must do.' I asked her what she was talking about and all she could say was that I would know it when it came along. And this is it. This is the most important thing I need to do right now. I need to visit Miranda and talk to her. I need to hear what she has to say to me and I need to say some things to her."

Mr. Morgan looked me straight in the eye and I did not look away. Then he spoke. "But even if they are willing to let you visit, what good can come from it? Why would I even consider the possibility of causing her more pain?"

I slipped the fourth letter out of my pocket and passed it to him. He read it and then sat silently for at least a full minute. Then he looked up at me. And nodded.

Chapter 26

Perhaps you think that what I was about to do was illogical, crazy, or downright perverse. There were no heroics, no high–minded notions. No plan. I took one step at a time, guided by my gut instinct. Maybe there was some sense of charity involved. Or perhaps it was a feeling of guilt. I won't rule that out.

It's possible that by the time you finish this, you still won't understand exactly why things turned out the way they did. All I know is that a single event when I was sixteen changed my life forever. And two survivors of that event would never lead what most would call normal lives. The law has no real way of creating justice. There is crime and there is punishment. And what of the end results? It was a whole lot simpler perhaps (wrong but simpler) when people truly believed that the Devil made a person murder. If it was the Devil who made a person act, then there was no true guilt. But now we know different. We understand something of cause and effect. Something of human psychology and human emotion. We know how to accuse and prove guilt and how to convict. But we know so little about the healing process beyond that. And we don't know how to contain the widening circle of pain caused by the death of someone who is loved.

I believed that it was absolutely necessary for me to sit down and talk with Miranda. It took a while to accomplish. But her father was a lawyer. Once he was convinced, he pulled some strings. On a cool October morning, my parents drove me to Woodvale and were prepared to wait in the parking lot until my visit was complete.

"You sure you don't want to reconsider?" my father asked. He and my mom were one thousand percent opposed to my meeting with Miranda.

"I've thought about this a lot."

"I'm worried that seeing her might trigger something, Michael," my mother said. "You have plenty of reasons to hate her. What if you can't control your anger?"

"I don't hate her. I'm past that. I've prepared myself for this. I really have."

We'd been through all this before. But they needed to hear it again. What I could not express to them was the fact that I somehow felt that Miranda and I shared something that no one else shared. That we were alike. Both victims. Of what I don't know. If these were ancient days, I could call it fate. I didn't believe in such a simplistic idea. But the link between us, the bond, if you can call it that, was why I had to see her. She had expressed it in her letters.

I opened the car door and approached the gate to Woodvale Youth Correctional Facility. It was not an unpleasant looking place. The law had treated Miranda with some degree of respect. I identified myself to a man in uniform and he directed me to a brick building and then watched as I walked up the driveway a short distance and entered. Inside, I told a woman guard who I was and that I had clearance. She made me walk through a metal detector much like the ones they use at the airport and I had to empty my pockets. Then I was ushered into a nearby office.

A woman in a dark suit greeted me. "Hello, Michael. I'm Sharon Elgard."

"Hi."

"You know this is highly, highly unusual. I'm not at all sure we should permit this."

"I know. But thank you for allowing it."

She put her hands in the air. "We like to think we're in the business of rehabilitation. I always thought the word 'correction' was a misnomer. We can't *correct* anything. But we'd like to do something. So we learn from our mistakes and sometimes we try new things. You're the new thing."

I understood what she meant and, in an odd way, it made me a shade more comfortable with what I was doing. "I'm curious," I said. "Did you read her letters to me?"

"Yes. We still do that."

"And?"

"And that was why we gave in to her father's request. And here you are."

"How is Miranda?"

"She's had a hard time. She's no trouble to us. But she gets depressed."

"Has she tried to hurt herself?"

"I can't talk about that."

"When can I see her?"

"Now. She's in Building C. There is a secured visiting

room there. A guard will be in the room with you."

"Is that necessary?"

"It's the policy."

"Okay."

I arrived first. The room reminded me of the waiting room of a dentist's office, except for the single table in the middle. I was led inside by a woman in uniform who did not smile. I sat in a chair at the plain wooden table. And I waited.

The room was dead silent except for the humming of a ventilation fan. The fluorescent lighting was too bright. As I sat alone, I felt a momentary panic. My heart beat loudly in my ears and I began to irrationally fear that I would be kept here. I was inside again. I would not be free to leave.

And then the door opened and Miranda walked in with the guard behind her. I would not have recognized her had she passed me on the street. She walked past me and sat across the table from me. Her hair was short and she looked older. Much older. Her skin looked pale. I recognized the pain and hurt in her eyes. The woman guard sat down in a folding chair by the door. I decided that I would pretend this third person was not in the room. It was not necessary to keep secrets. I had already decided that whatever I had to say was no secret. I did not know for sure, but I thought that our conversation might be taped. And I didn't care.

"Hi, Miranda."

"Michael, thanks for coming." Her voice was a mere whisper.

"I couldn't have gotten in without your father's help."

"I know and you persuaded him. That's a hard thing to do."

"He was okay. Are you all right?"

"I'm here. I'm alive. This place is not so bad."

The grounds were a sharp contrast to Severton. This place was like a summer camp compared to that. But I wasn't here to share my thoughts on accommodations. "What made you write to me?"

"I did a lot of thinking. And I've had lots of counseling here. I kept thinking that somehow I would start to feel… better. But I don't. I keep hoping something within me will change today or tomorrow. But it doesn't. And

I don't know if it ever will."

"I've changed. I've moved on," I said. It was partly a lie. "So will you."

There was the first hint of a smile, a little girl smile. And in it, I recognized the teenage girl who had attracted my attention. "I'm sorry to hear about your grandmother."

That caught me off–guard. "How did you know?"

She looked a little embarrassed. "I read the obituaries in the newspaper. I'm not sure why."

"You have a lot of time on your hands," I said, trying to lighten things up.

"Like you, I finished my high school work. I graduated. But it was different from when we were in school."

"I'm sure it was." And I told her about my graduation–but not how I felt at it–and I told her about my job. I didn't mention anything about Nicole.

A hint of a smile again. "I never imagined you fixing cars."

"Neither did I." I held out my hands for her to see. There was still some grease under the fingernails and I showed her the calluses on my palms. It was then she reached out and touched my hands. She held them and looked down at the table.

"How come you don't hate me?" she said in a low voice.

I had no real answer to that except this. "I did for a while. And then I found it was crippling me. I tried to let it go for a long while. But couldn't. And then I realized one day that I had no choice. If I didn't let it go, it would destroy me. It almost did."

"But I was the reason you were in prison."

"And you were the reason I was released."

She looked up at me. "How long can you stay?"

"They told me an hour maximum."

"Will you come back again?"

"I don't know."

"Then there are some things I need to say. I don't know what you will think of them, but I need to say them while you are here. And I realize you may not come back. I realize I may never see you again."

She was still holding onto my hands. "They–someone–is probably listening," I said. "I don't think this is really private."

"It doesn't matter. Does it matter to you?"

"No," I said. "A lot of things don't matter to me

anymore." But as soon as the words were out, I realized they were cruel, although I did not intend them so.

She let go of my hands and sat back, straightened her back, tried to look me in the eyes, but then looked down at the table. "In your head, you go through the sequence of events over and over. And even though you lived them, it doesn't seem possible. It doesn't seem real."

I nodded.

"Now I can see every bad decision that led up to what I did. The drugs were an important part of it but it wasn't just the drugs. When I started getting heavier into the meth, you backed off."

"I didn't like what it was doing to you. Or me."

"Where did that come from? How come you could see that and I couldn't?"

"I'm not sure. Something in me. Something from my parents and maybe from my grandmother. It sounds funny to say that since we were both trying so hard to be... what? Bad?"

"Yes. Bad. And we liked it, didn't we?"

"We loved it," I said. And just then I felt embarrassed because I was thinking of the sex we had. The bad/good sex.

The reckless sex that was so good. "But I loved you too. I'm sure of that now."

"So why did you give up on me?" she said suddenly, turning the tables. "Why didn't you help me?"

It was like a hammer to my head. "I tried," I said with defiance. "I tried to get you to ease up but you wanted to go further. So I moved on."

"There's that phrase again. Moved on."

"I did try to get you to see what was happening. I really did."

Her eyes were tearful. She took a breath, looked at me. With an air of defeat she said, "I know you did. In retrospect, I could see you tried to get me to slow down once I started in with the crystal meth every day. It was just that it was so cheap, so available, and so, so good. At first."

"It was addictive."

"Then how come you didn't stay with it?"

I threw up my hands. "Something within me saw the danger."

"When I saw you with Lisa... what?... two weeks after we broke up..."

"I didn't even think of it as breaking up. We just

drifted apart."

"No. It was much more than that."

"And that was the part I missed. Back then."

"I hated you at first," she said.

"But you were always with–what was his name?–Glenn and his friends. So I assumed…"

"You assumed that I had *moved on.*"

"Yes."

"They were part of the problem. Totally into the coke and the amphetamines, and they really liked the meth when I introduced them to it. But for Glenn, it was mostly about the sex."

I took a breath. "I don't think it was just sex between us, was it?"

"I think it was a big part of it. We were both really into it. But you treated me with respect."

"There's a funny word."

"Well, I don't know what else to call it. But then I hurt so badly when you stopped seeing me. And then started going out with Lisa."

I decided I would not talk about Lisa. Whatever I could say would be hurtful. I let Miranda continue.

"Here's the part I need to tell you. I'm not trying to say it was your fault in any way and I'm not trying to say it was just the drugs. But I want you to hear this. The sequence of events."

Something about the way her voice shifted. She was almost clinical and I knew she was about to tell me something about the actual murder. I wasn't sure I was prepared for that. "Sequence of events? You make it sound like someone else did it."

"No. I didn't mean that. Please. Will you listen to this part?"

I felt a chill and my heart began to pound again. Would I have come here had I known she was going to drag me through this? Night after night in prison and after, I had tried to erase the image of Lisa's death from my thoughts. Only now was it somewhat buried and rarely surfaced to surprise me awake or asleep. Miranda was breathing faster now. "Okay," I said, thinking that now I could handle it. And once she had said whatever she was about to say, I would walk out the door. Go to my parents' car in the parking lot and never return here again. "Go ahead."

"I hadn't slept for possibly four straight days. Once you're really into the meth, you just keep going. It got me through the day at school. I was planning on sleeping through the entire weekend. How's that for a plan? Now you know what the buzz from the meth feels like. Very high, very wired. Makes you sometimes feel strong and invulnerable. Then, other times, you get weird. Stressed. Paranoid. I thought people were following me. Glenn was no help. He and his buddies were also already moving on. I could sense that.

"Then I became obsessed with you. I believed—and maybe this part is true–that I still loved you. That I *really* loved you. And you had burned me off. Just walked away. And that Lisa girl. Too pretty. Too nice. I didn't really know her but I thought I knew her type. Smart. Wants to save the world. One of the gifted ones. I hated her. I was jealous. It seemed like the only thing I could depend on was the meth. The high.

"I tried to shut off the anger and hate that was growing, but I couldn't. I started carrying a knife–one I'd taken from my father's collection. And I followed you two one day. To that tent in the woods. And I watched."

I think my breath stopped just then. This was the very part that haunted me the most. Lisa and I in the tent with the flap open and only the screen between us and the outside world. And someone–Miranda–outside, watching us make love. "And then I left her there alone," I said. "I went home."

"She fell asleep," Miranda said.

I closed my eyes. I was almost afraid she was going to say: *and it was easy*–but she did not.

"At the time, and I know this sounds insane, at the time, I felt justified. That is what meth can do to you. I thought only about not getting caught. I got rid of the knife. I believed I could get away with it. When I realized they had arrested you, I believed you too were getting what you deserved."

"So while I was being accused of murder, you were doing what? Still getting high and feeling okay about what you did?"

"Not exactly. I did crash on the weekend. My body just couldn't take it. My father finally caught on and put me in detox. It was horrible getting off the stuff. But I kept my mouth shut about Lisa."

"All the way up to the time you finally confessed."

"I should have done it much sooner."

"But you didn't."

Miranda sat silently for at least a full minute. "Lately I've thought about ending my life."

"I know. That's part of why I'm here."

"I can't get rid of my past. I can't seem to think about much else and it wouldn't matter if I was in here or out in the world. It seems like a way out."

I truly understood what she was feeling. I'd felt it myself. Believed it was the only way to get past all the pain. The only true way to move on. "Why haven't you?" I asked, perhaps a bit too clinically.

"Because I wanted to see you. I wanted to talk with you."

"And I'm supposed to talk you out of it, right?"

"I don't know what you are supposed to do. Like I said, I'm responsible for what I did."

I looked at her. "It's funny. Lisa and I once debated capital punishment. Strangely enough, she was the one who believed it was better than long–term imprisonment and isolation from the world. I believed that life was sacred. A life for a life was too primitive. Then, when I was in prison, I came to the conclusion she was right. It was the humane way to end a cycle of pain and suffering."

"Then you understand why I wrote to you about wanting to end it."

"Yeah. I understand."

I nodded towards the guard and up at the ceiling. "So if they're listening, they'll know. They'll stop you."

"They already know." She lifted the long sleeve of the blouse and showed me the scars on her arm. Both arms.

"Jesus," I said out loud. And that's when it began to sink in. My own feelings of anger and frustration with the entire world. Not at Miranda. It wasn't her. It was an irrational, gut–wrenching rage at everything else. You feel fragments of this when you are a kid and especially a teenager. You get flashes of it later in life but if you've been through what I've been through, you sometimes feel a confirmation that it is truly a horrible screwed–up mess, this world we live in. And I realized at that very instant that I could not handle the final loss of Miranda. Defiance is what I felt. I felt a powerful defiance of the way things are.

"I'll be back for another visit," I said. "Will you be here?"

"Do you want me to be here?"

"Yes. I need you to be here."

She rolled both sleeves of her blouse back down and she looked directly at me and whispered, "Then I'll be here. I promise."

Chapter 27

Turning twenty–one in our culture is often considered a truly significant event in life. Last week we had a quiet party–just my parents and me at their house. Miranda was not invited. My parents have never adjusted to our decision to live together upon her release from Woodvale.

No matter how many times I've tried to explain it or make sense of it to just about anyone, but my parents in particular, I fail to get it right. Why this had to be. Even I don't really understand it. Let's call it a further sequence of events. Even as I write this in the most truthful manner I possibly can, I cannot quite make that sequence of events make sense to the world around me. Louis understands. I think. But no one else.

Our life together has, in many ways, cut us off from much of our past. Her parents do not accept me. Mine do not accept her. Lisa's mother and father think I have betrayed them. Her father went so far as to ask the police to look into the death of their daughter again. Presumably to see if there was some bizarre conspiracy. The events surrounding Lisa's death were reviewed by a committee that determined not to reopen the case.

But it means that even more people out there believe I was responsible for the death of a wonderful young woman who would have contributed so much to the world. I have to live with the fact of knowing what others believe, even if it is false. Miranda has to live with the fact that others know the truth. Both of us share a burden.

Let me take you back to then. And I will bring you up to now.

I returned to visit Miranda a second time. She was afraid I would not come back but now she began to trust me. When I e-mailed Nicole about my visits, she said she could never speak to me again. And she has been unwavering on that point.

I began to look forward to my visits with Miranda. We no longer spoke at all of the past. She was starting to feel better about herself. I was allowed one monthly visit and my parents protested each and every time. I understood that I was sacrificing them along the way. I knew how much they disapproved of what I was doing and I had to accept that. I moved on.

And what was it exactly that I was doing?

I was trying to figure out a way to live my life. From there on. And I believed that Miranda held the key. I could not go back anywhere and pick up the thread of where my old life had left off. I remembered that thing people said to me when I had been released: "Now you have your life back." It rang false even then.

Now I have *a* life.

Not an easy one. Or a happy one. But a life, nonetheless.

I still don't know why I walked away from the drugs when I did. And why Miranda could not. Something in me was different. Stronger. I still got high. But not on meth. In talking with Miranda in Woodvale, I began to understand what the old saying meant. *There but for the grace of God*. Or Fate. Or Luck. Or Circumstance. I grew to understand that a few more steps in the wrong direction and I too could have been a murderer.

And here's the point you don't want to hear: So could you. So could anyone.

So you are lucky that the sequence of events in your life have led you to where you are now. Quietly sitting somewhere, reading a book. A story that is very real but presented as fiction.

And maybe you still can't comprehend how I ended up in a relationship with Miranda. With someone who murdered the girl I loved. Maybe words can't do the job I want them to do. Maybe you just have to accept it. Accept it as a possibility in the realm of infinite possibilities.

What is it you require to get on with your life every day? Draw up a list. It may or may not make sense to others when you show it to them.

But top on my list is this. I need Miranda to be in my life. I need to help her. And I need to do this for me.

Miranda turned twenty–one before I did. At her parole hearing, she was given an extraordinary decision. After the petitions from her father, the pleadings of her counselors, and an eloquent but heartbreaking letter from Miranda herself, she was set free on her twenty–first birthday. But there was no birthday party. She insisted on that.

She went home first. And I was not permitted to visit her. But we had already planned on renting an apartment and moving in together. I had been attending night classes at the community college and preparing myself for what is known as "human services." The classes were a little dull but I completed the program. I would work as an assistant with kids with disabilities and with troubled kids. I would be a "youth worker," a term I never liked.

It was tough at first. Given my background, who would hire me? But then someone gave me a break. A friend of my old high school principal, Mr. Tyson, interviewed me as a favor for Tyson. I was hired to work in a group home. I stayed there three nights a week. I dealt with some nasty kids with bad attitudes who did not fit into society. I didn't really like most of them. But I thought I understood them a bit, enough to keep a lid on the situation. Enough to listen to them when they wanted to talk. Enough to keep them–sometimes–from doing the next stupid thing.

And I rented my own one bedroom apartment in an old converted house. No cable TV. No high–speed Internet. And I read at night. My book collection continued to grow. I read the *Bible* another time and found things in it–passages of wisdom I had missed because my vision was clouded.

I liked *Proverbs*, and the *Book of Job* had new meaning. And I liked the teachings of Jesus but not the familiar story of his life nor the way it was told.

My grandmother's famous *I Ching* remained helpful. I had almost memorized many of the meanings of the hexagrams but was especially fond of the pairing of Hexagram 33 and Hexagram 35.

Thirty–three (*Tun*) represents retreat and reads: *Once you decide to retreat, do so with determination. If you do it with regret, you will not succeed.* Thirty–five (*Chin*) suggests: *Greet obstruction and objection with an open and generous mind but trust must be earned as well.*

Placed between them is Thirty–four (*Ta Chuang*) known as the hexagram of great strength. *Going forward with care and caution will bring positive results. Obstacles disappear.* That is the hexagram that represents my grandmother to me. I still miss her and know she would be saddened by seeing the distance that has grown between my parents and me.

Shortly before Miranda was released, I moved into this apartment. I furnished it with used and donated furniture from my parents and their friends. It was a kind of conspiracy between Miranda and me. This plan to live together. I cannot say how difficult it was, knowing this would add more pain to the lives of my own parents.

I am away some nights working at the group home. Miranda says she does not sleep on those nights, but waits until I return and then sleeps through the day.

She said she too would like to help people and take a certificate in "human services," but her criminal record will not allow for that under any circumstances. So she is mulling over what other course of action to take. I tell her not to hurry. I think something will present itself–an important opportunity. "Keep an open mind," I say, quoting my grandmother's favorite expression.

But my parents do not like for me to say that. "Look at what you are doing," my mother says. "This can't be right."

And so, my twenty–first birthday party was not a party but a solemn occasion for parents who believed they had lost a son. And me? I still love my parents but I could not do what they wanted. All I could say was, "This is how I can get on with my life." No one gave me back my life. I had to create a new one.

I know what you are thinking, what you are wondering: Do you love her? Does she love you?

And to those questions there is no easy answer. I can say that it is important that we are with each other. We have a relationship that is essential. We need each other. I know that. Something may change some day, I am aware of that. But I don't spend much time thinking about the future. To the best of my ability I live in the here and now.

And what I know of love changes over time. We do not say, "I love you" to each other, if that helps to explain things. But at the same time, I want to tell you that I care deeply about Miranda. She is kind and appreciative with me and still in "retreat" from the outer world. I am two hexagrams ahead. I have "advanced" but I missed the in–between step, the hexagram of inner strength. I'm still working on that one.

But love. Do I "love" her? I don't know if I can answer that.

The word has been so corrupted that it may no longer have meaning.

But no. I am sidestepping.

Love was what I felt for Lisa.

And I cannot fully connect Lisa to Miranda in a way that makes sense. What came in between? Pain and suffering and waiting for things to get better.

Miranda and I have never made love since she was released. Whenever we've discussed the possibility, we pull back and decide it isn't important. Or so we say.

But I do hold her in my arms at night as we sleep together. She misses me when I am gone and I miss her. I cook meals for her with pride. (Louis taught me to be a great cook.) And sometimes she prepares food for me and takes care of the apartment.

And when we wake together on a sunlit morning, one of us will say that we are "lucky to have each other." And then we may even laugh.

And at such times the world is not such a terrible place after all. It has given us permission to get on with our lives as best we can. And I am convinced that this is enough.